ZORA *and* ME

ZORA AND ME

VICTORIA BOND

and

T. R. SIMON

CANDLEWICK PRESS

Copyright © 2010 by Victoria Bond and T. R. Simon

First edition 2010

Library of Congress Cataloging-in-Publication Data

Bond, Victoria, date.

Zora and me / by Victoria Bond and T. R. Simon.

p.   cm.

Summary: A fictionalized account of Zora Neale Hurston's childhood with her best friend, Carrie, in Eatonville, Florida, as they learn about life, death, and the differences between truth, lies, and pretending. Includes an annotated bibliography of the works of Zora Neale Hurston, a short biography of the author, and a time line of important events in her life.

Includes bibliographical references

ISBN 978-0-7636-4300-3

1. Hurston, Zora Neale — Childhood and youth — Juvenile fiction.

[1. Hurston, Zora Neale — Childhood and youth — Fiction.

2. Coming of age — Fiction. 3. Race relations — Fiction.

4. African Americans — Fiction. 5. Eatonville (Fla.) — History —

20th century — Fiction.] I. Simon, T. R. (Tanya R.) II. Title.

PZ7.B63693Zo 2010

[Fic] — dc22   2009047410

10 11 12 13 14 15 RRC 10 9 8 7 6 5 4 3 2 1

Printed in Crawfordsville, IN, U.S.A.

This book was typeset in Centaur.

Candlewick Press

99 Dover Street

Somerville, Massachusetts 02144

visit us at www.candlewick.com

For Charles Biot, the storyteller. For Dolores Biot, the reader.

V. B.

This book is for Richard Jonathan Simon
and
Viviana Mireille Gardis Simon.
They are my beauty and my truth.

T. R. S.

CHAPTER ONE

I t's funny how you can be in a story but not realize until the end that you were in one. Zora and I
entered our story one Saturday two weeks before
the start of fourth grade.

That Saturday, while our mamas were shopping,
Zora and I were sitting under the big sweet gum tree
across the road from Joe Clarke's storefront making
sure we were in earshot of the chorus of men that
perched on his porch. We sat under the tree, digging
our feet into the rich dark soil, inviting worms to
tickle us between the toes. We pretended to be talking and playing with the spiky monkey balls that had

fallen from the sweet gum branches, but we were really listening to the menfolk's stories and salty comments and filing them away to talk about later on. That's when Sonny Wrapped strolled up in his Sunday suit, strutting like he owned the town and not just a pair of new pointy shoes, and calling for folks to come watch him whup a gator.

Sonny was a young welder from Sanford who had come to Eatonville to court Maisie Allard. For three weekends straight, he'd been wooing her with sweet talk and wildflowers. When he wasn't with her, he was shooting his mouth off about how tough he was. That particular day, Sonny had managed to track down the king of the gators, the biggest and oldest one in Lake Maitland, Sanford, or Eatonville. The gator's name was Ghost, and for good reason. One minute he was sunning on a mud bank or floating in the pond, his back exposed like a twenty-foot-long banquet of rocks; the next minute he'd have disappeared, and the pond would be as still as a wall.

Anyway, Sonny got a couple dozen men to walk the short distance to Lake Hungerfort to watch him wrestle the gator. Zora's father, her eldest brother, Bob, and Joe Clarke were among them. Nobody was thinking about the two of us, but we still had sense enough to lag behind and make ourselves invisible. Everyone stood a good ways back from the lake—close enough to see but far enough to have time to scoot up a tree if Sonny lost control.

Ghost lay still as death, but as Sonny approached, his eyes were like two slow-moving marbles. Before Sonny could jump Ghost from behind, the old gator swung his tail around and knocked Sonny off his feet.

To this day, I can still see Joe Clarke running toward Sonny, yelling, "Roll! Roll!" If Sonny could tumble out of the reach of Ghost's jaws, he might have a chance.

But Sonny was too stunned to get his mind around Ghost's cunning. He gaped, wide-eyed and mute, as the gator clamped down on his arm and dragged him into the water.

People began to scream. I think I remember screaming myself. One thing I remember for sure is Zora, just standing and watching without a sound, tears streaming down her face.

Joe Clarke is a big man, but he hesitated for a second—a grown man paying respect to his fear—before diving into the water. Two other brave men—Mr. Hurston and Bertram Edges, the blacksmith—dove in a moment later.

It took the three of them to drag Sonny back on dry ground. I'll never know how. They were bruised like prizefighters. But they were better off than Sonny, whose arm had been mangled past all recognition.

Back in our homes, we chewed on silence and thought about Dr. Pritchard, awake all night trying to patch up Sonny and make him right.

The next morning, Joe Clarke rode to all the churches in his capacity as town marshal and gave the pastors the news: Sonny didn't make it.

For two weeks after that, you would see pairs of grim men with shotguns scouring the ponds for a sign of Ghost, but they found nothing.

In the days that followed, Zora's father said it "wasn't fitting" to talk about what had happened to Sonny in front of women and children. Even Joe Clarke, who loved a story better than almost anyone, refused to talk about Sonny and Ghost.

Sometimes when I think back on that steamy afternoon, I can see my own father emerging soaking wet from Lake Hungerfort, Sonny's broken body in his arms. But that was impossible, because my daddy had already been gone six months by then. And that's another reason I remember that summer so clear: it was the summer my mama gave up believing my daddy would come home. She had cried just about all a person can cry.

As for Zora, while every kid in the schoolyard could talk of nothing else for days and pestered Zora and me for eyewitness reports, she quietly closed in on Sonny's death, like an oyster on a bit of sand. A week later, she had finally turned that bit of sand into a storied pearl.

CHAPTER TWO

I am not lying!" Zora shot at Stella Brazzle.

Zora and me and our friend Teddy were facing Stella Brazzle and her gang—Hennie, Joanne, and Nella. They were jealous of the attention kids showered on me and Zora for having been right at the spot when Sonny met his fate.

All four of those girls (Brazzles, as we called them among ourselves) were daughters of professional men—a doctor, a dentist, a tailor, and an undertaker. This meant more to them than it did to us; to hear them talk, you would have thought they were the duchesses and countesses and princesses of Eatonville.

They carried themselves like every day was Easter.
Nearly all the other girls would have liked to be them,
and the older boys were always buzzing around them.
And the more it happened, the more the Brazzles were
the focus of every eye, the more they believed that they
should be the focus of every eye.

"You are too lying," Stella snapped. "You the
lyingest girl in town! You so lying, even when you tell
the truth, it comes out a lie!"

"He turned into a half gator," Zora insisted. "And
I saw it—I was there!"

Recess had just started, and our whole class was
gathered in a tight half circle before Zora. Stella hated
sharing the spotlight with anyone, but especially with
Zora.

Stella Brazzle crossed her arms and smirked.
"Where was this, Zora? Top of a magic bean-stalk?"

Everyone laughed except for Teddy and me. We
exchanged a look and then looked protectively at
Zora. She didn't notice us. Her eyes were focused on
her audience.

"I'm gone tell y'all just how it happened from the
very beginning," Zora said.

"Don't nobody wanna hear your ol' lies," Stella
Brazzle barked. "Ain't that right, y'all?" Not a soul

moved or uttered a word—not even the Brazzles. Zora took that as a cue to begin. Everyone was eager for a story, and we all knew that nobody could tell a story better than Zora.

"I finished up my chores early last night so I could go out on the porch and catch fireflies over at the Blue Sink." Fireflies are so thick there at night, you can just put out your arm and they'll land on it. You don't even have to try to catch them. "I couldn't have been there more than ten minutes, and I'd already filled my jar, when I heard a strange whistling sound."

You could hear us holding our breath, it was so quiet.

"What kinda whistling?" Ralph Hardiman asked, his eyebrows raised like clothespins were keeping them up.

"Strange-sounding, not like any bird or person I ever heard make," Zora said. "But that wasn't the worst of it. The night started getting dark and misty, and the fireflies started disappearing. Soon I couldn't make out a thing in front of me until I got near Mr. Pendir's house."

"Then what happened?" Teddy and I asked in unison.

"I was surrounded by white fog, but not thick like

clouds. Nuh-uh. It was stringy—like spiderwebs!"
She suddenly waved her fingers at us like they were
daddy longlegs, and half the circle jumped back. But
nobody laughed.

"Then, as fast as it started, the spiderweb fog disappeared. I was flat on my belly in wet grass, right
close up to Mr. Pendir's porch, in the dark. I didn't
even realize I'd gotten that close. I lay there for a long
minute, still as a stone, trying to steady my eyes on the
glowy light inside the house."

Half a dozen voices: "What you see?"

"The screen door swung open." Zora paused for
effect. "Out of the light stepped Mr. Pendir. But
where his nose and mouth should have been, he had a
long, flat gator snout!"

"A gator snout?" we all shouted—even Stella
Brazzle, in spite of herself.

Zora nodded slowly. "That's right," she said. "Mr.
Pendir looked like a gator man—man body, gator
head! That's his secret. And *that's* how come can't no
gator kill him!"

One thing about gators that folks outside our
parts don't usually know is that they make loud hissing sounds. Not all the time—only when one of their
young is in trouble. It's a call to arms, and it sounds

like a cross between birthing pains and dying pains. Mr. Pendir, a carpenter by trade, just like Zora's father, was fishing in Amherst Lake one time in a tiny dugout canoe that he had built himself, when he accidentally cornered a young gator. An older gator caught sight of this and started up that horrible hissing. Mr. Pendir, no fool, knew exactly what it meant. Next thing he knew, *three* grown gators were in the water and swimming his way. But he didn't panic — not the way I heard it told. He let the gators get close to his boat, then threw the bucketful of fish he'd caught right at them. It distracted them just long enough for him to jump in the water and swim like the dickens to shore. The three gators smashed his boat to pieces, but Mr. Pendir lived to tell the tale, without a scratch on his peanut-colored bald head.

If any other man in the town had survived the same experience, he would have crowed about it all over creation. Not Mr. Pendir. No one would have known about it at all if Joe Clarke hadn't seen him carving a new canoe and asked him what happened to the old one. Everyone knew Mr. Pendir to be quiet and honest, and no one doubted the story for a minute. Still, some folks ran to the lake anyway and found the splintered pieces of the dugout canoe washed up on the shore. All of Eatonville looked at Mr. Pendir a little funny after that. So it didn't seem so far-fetched that Mr. Pendir could actually be what Zora said he was, half gator and half man.

"Well . . . *then* what happened?" Stella Brazzle snapped the question, angry at herself for being curious.

"What do you think? I jumped up and ran! But the whole way home, I could hear the creaking sound of a gator opening its jaws and clapping them shut."

Teddy blinked. "Did he follow you?" he asked, nervous, like it had just occurred to him that Mr. Pendir might be gaining on Zora and the rest of us, even now.

Zora didn't have a chance to respond. Our teacher, Mr. Calhoun, stepped out onto the stoop of the schoolhouse and rang the bell. The spell was broken. As we all ran inside, kids shouted things like, "Aw, fibber," "You crazy, Zora," and, "You ain't seen no such thing!"

"All right, don't believe me, then," Zora said. "But when all y'all coulda been playing kickball, you were standing around like boards listening to me. That alone is proof I'm telling the truth." And she beamed, as proud as if they had given her a medal for bravery.

The rest of the day, I paid maybe half attention to the lessons at best. Zora had cast a long shadow over my favorite swimming hole. There's a lot of places in and around Eatonville where you can have a swim, but Blue Sink—barely bigger around than a big house but deep enough that it never dried up—was ours. At the deepest end, an old weeping willow dipped in the water like a braided head, and we would swing out on its strong vines before letting go at just the right instant. Those moments of flying in the air before the water swallowed us in one cool gulp were pure joy, and I hated to think they were over.

But I also couldn't stop thinking about what Zora had said. Just because something's good listening doesn't necessarily make it true, and Zora didn't have any trouble telling a fib or stretching a story for fun. I could tell that Zora herself believed the story, but the question was, did I?

By the time three o'clock finally came, it was so hot that I convinced myself it was all foolishness. The three of us had been swimming at the Blue Sink since forever, and with the heat probably pressing up to one hundred degrees, I was willing to take my chances. I just had to have a dip.

CHAPTER THREE

Zora was walking beside me, eyeing me. "You sure?" she kept asking. "You sure you want to go to Blue Sink after what I seen last night?"

Each time she asked, I grew more determined. "I'm fixing to turn into molasses if I don't."

"Well," she said, "I guess if it's two of us, maybe he won't try anything. . . ."

I had a pang of wishing Teddy was with us, but I didn't say anything. Teddy always had to run home after school and do his chores on the farm before he could come out and join us.

Zora continued. "Mr. Pendir probably don't show his gator head in the day, anyway." Even though she'd had the wits scared out of her the night before, she didn't want to give up the Blue Sink, either.

Spanish moss hung low over the pond like layers of gray-fringed blankets. Woodpecker and nuthatch beckoned us with snare drum *rat-a-tat-tat* and *whee-hyah*. Zora was the first to drop her books and strip down to her underclothes. I was a few beats slower, making sure to keep Mr. Pendir's house in plain sight.

Zora ran toward the red cliff of dirt over the water but stopped short, and I almost ran into her. Someone was sitting on the ledge, fishing. When she called out, her voice crackling like hot chicken grease, I knew exactly who it was. "Y'all children run like you woke up itching to topple an old lady over!" Old Lady Bronson cried. "Just itching."

We would be lucky to escape the afternoon without getting a spell hurled at us.

Zora's voice was calm. "We didn't mean any harm."

Old Lady Bronson jerked her head to the side, flashing us her pinched profile, and her thick gray braid whipped between her shoulder blades like a long tail.

"Zora Neale Hurston," Old Lady Bronson said,

"please don't tell me what you meant and what you didn't mean. My first two names ain't Old Lady for nothing. I been round here as long as there's *been* a *round here*. Now, git! Go on. Git! I want my peace. And old ladies should have what they want."

Zora put her hand on her hip. Old Lady Bronson might get what she wanted that afternoon, but she was also going to get something from Zora.

"If you're not careful, Old Lady Bronson," she warned, "Mr. Pendir is gonna get you! You might be a roots woman, but Mr. Pendir, he can take on the face of a gator! And here you are sitting all alone near his house. That ain't safe for nobody, much less an old lady."

"What you say, child? Pendir, a gator?" Old Lady Bronson laughed. "Girl, what folks say 'bout you is all wrong. You ain't a *liar*—you just crazy as a hoot owl! The powerful ones be the little old ladies. Ain't a soul in this town can match me for strength if the test don't require lifting a finger."

Everyone knew that Old Lady Bronson made spells—plenty went to her to get their broken hearts patched up or have a whammy taken off. But few got to hear her say out loud that she had conjure power. It sent the cold tingles running up my back.

But Zora wasn't fazed a bit.

"All I'm saying is, you better watch out, if you want to keep your arms and legs," Zora said.

"You don't got to worry 'bout me, small fry. What you need to worry the hair off your head 'bout is getting un-crazy." Old Lady Bronson laughed.

Once I heard a man on Joe Clarke's porch say that Old Lady Bronson came from a long line of mean and kept a long line going. She had four daughters, all of them my mama's age or older, and they were all mean. The youngest of them, Miss Eunice, was so mean that after she was grown and living way up by Pensacola, she came to visit Old Lady Bronson one time to borrow her mule, and took the mule but left her own little girl, Billie, who couldn't have been more than five at the time. Old Lady Bronson had to raise Billie up herself, even though she was already an old lady. When Billie started to get grown, Old Lady Bronson taught her midwifery and, for some reason, Billie is the only Bronson woman who didn't come out mean.

Zora rolled her eyes and turned her back on the old lady. I backed away so the old lady couldn't cast any hoodoo dust at us while we weren't looking.

Zora casually picked up her clothes, shoes, and books. "Who wants to go swimming, anyway?" she said, loud enough so Old Lady Bronson could hear. "There's lots better things we could do."

I agreed. I couldn't think of any at the moment, but I was glad for an excuse to get away from the Blue Sink. Between Mr. Pendir's gator head and Old Lady Bronson's juju, 200 degrees couldn't make me want to swim there now.

CHAPTER FOUR

As we were leaving, we heard cracking twigs and looked up to see Teddy in his overalls, come to find us after his chores.

"How come y'all ain't swimming?"

Zora motioned over her shoulder. "Old Lady Bronson."

Teddy needed no more explanation than that and fell in step with us. "Better things to do than swimming, anyways," he said.

Zora slowed to a stroll, letting her hands graze the pines on either side of us. "That's what I just told Carrie. Lots better things."

"Such as . . . ?" I asked.

"Well, there's always—" Zora looked to Teddy, as if they'd planned that he was going to finish her sentence.

Teddy seemed so startled by the responsibility that all of us burst out giggling. Then he got a funny look, like he was trying to decide something. "There is one thing. . . ."

"What?"

"What?"

"Mm . . ." He looked back and forth between us. "I might could show you something, but you have to keep it a secret. Folks can't know about it."

The word *secret* got our immediate attention, and we swore oaths from this life to the next that we would never, ever, on pain of death, reveal whatever it was that Teddy knew but hadn't yet shared with us.

"Come on, then." He took us on the shortcut he always used to get from the farm to Blue Sink, though I never did understand how he followed it because there was no path to follow. The path was in his head; he just knew which spaces to press through.

"Look out for the bramble," Teddy said over his shoulder. He looked as serious as a preacher on a Sunday, and the more we begged him to tell us what we were on our way to see, the more serious he became. Still, there was something else in his grave face that made me think he didn't mind us begging and begging him, that he might even be enjoying it.

Zora and I couldn't stop grinning like it was Christmas. Teddy had shared a secret like this before only twice in our lives, and each time it was something that filled us with wonder for weeks. If Teddy thought something was worth keeping secret, then it most surely was.

Teddy slithered under the twisty trunk of a big fallen cottonwood tree, and we slithered under right after him. Then he spun around to look at us with big eyes, his finger to his lips.

We froze. Teddy crouched down. We crouched down. Teddy duckwalked over to a chinquapin, and we duckwalked over to it, too. Teddy knelt and pointed through a hole in the branches, cautioning us with another sign for *Silence!*

We peered through the branches. Under the starry leaves, a little ways past us — maybe twenty feet or so — there was . . . something. It was dark and bristly and sort of moving. No, not really moving. Sort of . . . shaking? A bear? No, not a bear — it was long but too narrow to be a bear, and it was making a kind of grunty, humming sound.

I squinched my eyes, and I suddenly knew. It was a razorback! A big mama razorback pig. And what I had thought was her shaking was a squirming litter of at least a dozen piglets, all rooting and snorting and squinking to get at the mama's teats while she just lay there with her eyes closed, grunting a little every now and then.

Zora pinched my arm — we were both trying to keep from squealing with pleasure. She was beaming so wide and bright, there was hardly anything left of her face but smile.

Teddy was still kneeling behind us, grinning like it was his babies all squirming and ernking behind the chinquapin. He just nodded for us to keep looking, and we didn't need a second nudge. Zora and I kept watching the wondrous sight, poking each other every time one of the piglets got jostled out of place, like one of us might miss it.

The surprise shouldn't have surprised me, really, because nobody cared more for animals than Teddy did. He had names for every creature on the farm. Lots of farm kids do that, but Teddy could also tell you about their personalities, what they liked and didn't like, how to calm them down when they got worked up, and more. And an animal didn't have to be on the farm to get Teddy's care—he was always finding birds or squirrels or rabbits that were sick or hurt. He tried to help them when he could, and when he couldn't, he gave them decent burials. Once in a long while Teddy found the remains of a creature long passed, and he would clean up the bones and put them on his windowsill, where he had a small but wonderful trove of skulls and shells.

I found myself staring at the tusks of the mama and had a shiver of fear—if she saw us, she could charge us. But then I thought about how Teddy had probably come this close a bunch of times, letting her get used to his smell so she knew that he didn't pose a threat.

We must have watched for close on to half an hour, and would have kept on watching if the mama hadn't started to stir. Teddy tapped us on the shoulders, gave us the *Silence!* sign again, and motioned for us to move back the way we had come. We did our best, and I guess we did OK, since the steady grunting and sucking of the pigs just kept right on going.

Once we got back past the bramble, Teddy figured we were far enough away to talk without worrying about waking the mama razorback.

But before he could say a word, we were giving him a big old hug and just laughing and laughing. He still wore that serious look, but there was a proud little smirk around the corner edge of his mouth, too.

"Did you see the little runty one that kept getting pushed away?"

"Yeah, but he's a fighter, that one. He's scrappy."

"Why you so sure it's a boy?"

"Well, 'cause —"

"Yeah, why? Girls can fight good, too!"

"That's right!"

We pushed Teddy down onto the pine needles and tickled him so he couldn't catch his breath, much less fight back. Though now that I think about it, Teddy could always fight back when he had to. I guess he just didn't want to. And, really, we weren't trying to show him what good fighters we were. It was that we had so much joy in him — he could be such a boy with the boys yet so gentle with animals, and he shared the best of everything he had with nobody but us: Zora and me.

He finally said uncle, and we let him up.

"So remember to mind what you say about girls now," we said.

Teddy was still laughing, brushing needles off his overalls and trying to shake them out from inside. "Yeah, y'all pretty tough," he said, rolling his eyes. Before we could say something back, he got all serious again. "Listen, y'all got to promise again never to tell anybody ever about them pigs."

We looked back at him just as serious. "Teddy, we already promised you. And we don't never break a promise."

He shook his head. "I know, but I'm just . . . If anybody finds out—if my daddy or my brothers ever find out"—he almost winced—"they'll come here and kill 'em. All of 'em!"

If my face was half as stricken as Zora's, you would have thought the babies were mine.

"But why?"

"How could they do that?"

Teddy jammed his hands in his pockets. "My daddy says a razorback's a pest—dig up the dirt, feast on all the good eating birds, and don't even have good fatback if you kill it." He kicked up a cloud of dirt and needles. "But that don't mean you have to kill it."

Zora had a soft look. "We won't never tell nobody. Ain't that right, Carrie?"

"That's right. And I bet if the three of us keep it secret, won't nobody find out. Mama Pig'll raise all them squinky little piglets big and strong before anyone knows, and then won't nobody mess with 'em. Even the little runty one."

"Yeah," said Zora. "Can you imagine anyone picking a fight with a whole pack of wild razorbacks? I know I sure wouldn't!"

Teddy looked at us, looked away, and then looked at us again. "You right," he said. Then he looked at me while motioning to Zora. "Be pretty funny to see *her* try, though."

Zora laughed. "Shoot! We already done whupped your kettle for you—but you give me a mind to do it again!" And before Teddy could even think of a smart answer, she tripped him so he went sprawling back on the needles he'd worked so hard to shake off. Then she tore away, pulling me after her and calling, "Last one to the Loving Pine is a rotten egg!"

We hadn't gotten a dozen paces when Teddy took off yelling and raced right past us, like lightning was running right behind him. I tried my best to be lightning.

CHAPTER FIVE

Zora had a way of giving personality to everything in Eatonville. Flowers alongside the road weren't just flowers. One day they were royal guards saluting us on our walks home. Another day they were God's consolation to the ground for putting it underfoot. That's how Zora saw things. Everything in the world had a soul, and soul to her meant being more than anyone counted on.

Even though the Loving Pine was a real-life tree, Zora made it much more than bark and branches and sweet needles, more than a beautiful longleaf pine. "Just because something can't talk," she said, "doesn't mean it can't give and get love." I don't think it ever meant to me and Teddy what it meant to her, but that didn't stop us from calling it the Loving Pine and treating it the way she did anyway.

Zora said the patch of rich moss under the branchy cover was a beautiful velvet blanket the tree had spread out for us, and when we lay ourselves down on it, we always said, "Thank you, Loving Pine," because we couldn't help feeling grateful. She also told us that the tree could feel, so we were careful never to hurt the Loving Pine's feelings. Zora said it could give hugs, so we sometimes knelt around its prickly trunk and gave it hugs back. If it hadn't been for Zora, we might never have given that tree a second look or singled it out from any of its neighbors. But we did, and we saw in bits and pieces what Zora saw all of the time.

"Now who's a rotten—?" Teddy said, but didn't finish his question. He had beat me and Zora to the tree by half a minute and just stood there staring at a man sitting under the far green awning of the Loving Pine, legs crossed, guitar in his lap, and blinking like we'd just woken him from a nice nap. Which I suppose we had.

The man smiled. It was a sunshineful smile, glinty and warm, not like Stella Brazzle's, which was wasted on the face of somebody so mean. But like my daddy's. The man's skin was almost the same color as his hair and his eyes, like somebody had poured dark honey all over him, then washed it off but left the color stuck on.

Without saying hello or waiting for us to say hello, he started to sing. He sang kind of dreamy, eyes half closed, head rolling slowly from one side to the other, like it was his way of waking up.

"Aw, when the day is done, it just gets lent away," he sang, strumming the guitar strung over his shoulder with a deep red braid of string. *"Mm, when the day is done, it just gets lent away. Ain't a thing gets gone, just goes somewheres else to stay . . ."*

He hadn't sung but two words when I knew. Whoever poured the honey on his skin had let it run all down his voice, too. For my part, it was his voice alone that won me over, even as his song made my eyes cry.

Zora couldn't contain her excitement. She loved meeting new people, especially traveling folks, and from his clothes, the singing man looked to be an itinerant turpentine worker, one of the many who came from all around to tap our pines each year.

When you live your life in a place where folks

hold home dearer than any treasure, you don't usually cotton to folks who like life on the road, even
less if the road took someone away from you. Zora
was different—she would hang off the fence in front
of her house, waving down cars and buggies passing
through Eatonville on their way to or from Winter
Park or Orlando. That didn't take a thing away from
her love for Eatonville, but from the top of her head
to the tips of her toes, Zora was a wanderer at heart.

"You got an awfully pretty voice, Mister," Zora
said. "I bet didn't nobody lend that to you."

The stranger smiled. "You got that right." He
took all three of us in with his eyes. "What are y'all
names? They yours to keep, or are they out on loan?"

We laughed and told him.

"Zora, Carrie, and Teddy."

"Ivory at your service," he replied, a single curl
plastered to his sweaty forehead.

"You a turpentine worker?" Teddy asked, a hint
of wariness in his voice.

Ivory patted the ground, inviting us to sit, and we
made a little crescent in front of him.

"Some days I am," he said. "Most days I'm just
me."

"You travel a lot?" That was always Zora's first

question for a stranger. In her mind, there wasn't anything more marvelous in this world than going to far-flung places. Or, if you couldn't get there yourself, hearing other people tell about it and then imagining it.

"I figure I done a little traveling. Been to Savannah, been to Atlanta, been to Washington City, been to —"

"What's the farthest place you ever been?" Zora was so animated, I could tell she'd already packed her bags and bought her ticket.

"Well, New York City got to be the —"

"New York City! You been to New York City?" For the next few minutes, Zora was shooting questions at Ivory like she was a popgun. He hardly got to finish a single answer before she went on to the next question, but he didn't mind being interrupted — just kept smiling that glowy smile and crinkling his eyes up in a way my daddy used to have. Finally he just bust out laughing, and even his laughing had music in it.

"What's so funny?" asked Zora, smiling in spite of herself. "Why you laughing? These important questions I'm asking!"

"Honey, I know they important, but you got a hundred times more than I'll ever have the answers to!

I think you need to go on up and visit New York City your own self!"

"I may just have to do that," Zora said. I could see that she'd lost her ticket for the moment, but her bags were still good and ready.

"I bet you will. You got the travelin' bug. Some folks just made to go out and see the world. They're like bees, spreading all kinds of pollen—gospel, news, stories, and songs. That's what makes travel so magical; everyone that moves around leaves little seeds of themselves behind." He strummed a chord and sang again:

"I went down to the gypsy
  To get my fortune told.
  She said what's lost is lost even if it's got a home.
  'Cause it's the looking and finding folks
  That feel most alone."

I couldn't help my curiosity and interrupted his song. "Mr. Ivory, are *you* a looking or finding folk?"

Ivory took a slow breath. "I reckon everyone's got someone they're looking to find. Sometimes the problem is trying to find somebody who don't know they lost or don't want to be found."

I felt like he had looked down my soul. I didn't think he would have known my father, but something about what he said made me want to hope.

My father wasn't a carpenter, like Zora's daddy, or a farmer, like Teddy's, but he was rangy and strong, and he loved to work hard. He always tried to find work nearby, but sometimes he had to "follow the pickin'," and just go wherever they needed hands. He could get work anytime at the turpentine camps around Lake Maitland, but Mama was scared for him to be with men like that. I never asked *Like what?*, but I knew it couldn't be good. It was the only thing I ever saw them even come close to disagreeing about; they liked each other more than any grown people I'd ever known, except maybe Teddy's parents — but even Teddy's mama and daddy never held hands like mine did.

The last time my parents had talked about turp work was last fall. My daddy heard they needed men for a third shift at the factories down in Orlando to make things in time for Christmas. It was three or four good weeks' work, but he would have to be away. It was either that or turpentine. So he went to Orlando. He never came back.

A month later, his cousin Leon went to Orlando to look for him. He asked around for days, but couldn't find anything—not even anyone who'd seen him or thought they might have seen him. Just nothing.

I got used to falling asleep to the sound of my mother weeping, but around the time Sonny Wrapped met that gator Ghost, she stopped. First I thought it was a good thing, even a good sign. Until I realized that she had stopped crying because she had stopped hoping. That's when a new kind of sadness settled on me and on our house like folks waiting for a train they know won't come.

"You been working turpentine down here a while?" I asked Ivory.

He cocked his head. "About a year or so . . ."

"Did you ever run across a man named Avery Brown? Little bigger than you, same color eyes as you, with a gentle manner?" I felt Zora and Teddy looking at me. "Did you ever know him?"

Ivory's face softened. "I never did know a man like that. I would have remembered him for sure if I did."

A dark cloud passed over Ivory's face for a quick second, then left as he strummed a bright chord. "I reckon it's like the song says. Nothing really ends. Even the spirits of folks don't never end. They just get lent away." He smiled, as if he meant his words to comfort us, but the sad look in his eyes said he wasn't sure he comforted himself, much less us.

Ivory stood up, stretched, and brushed himself off.

"Well, now, y'all . . . I think I hear some pine trees calling me to come take their sap before the sun sets. That's how I'll earn my nighttime dip in that sweet little swimming hole down the road."

Hearing him mention the Blue Sink, Zora frowned. "You want to be careful of . . . gators in these parts, Mr. Ivory."

Ivory laughed. "I've outlived creatures much more dangerous than old gators. But don't you worry. I'll keep my wits about me."

He adjusted his red guitar strap and headed for the road, strumming the same song and humming, his sweet moan like a trail of tears behind him.

CHAPTER SIX

It was getting on dinner, and we walked Teddy as far as his "path" before heading to the Hurston home, where I ate on Monday, Thursday, and Friday evenings. Zora had only to hit the first step on the porch of their eight-room house for her mama to know it was her. She often said that, of all of her children, Zora's footsteps sounded most like her own. Not many folks pay close attention to what their own footsteps sound like, but Lucy Hurston did.

"That Carrie you got with you?" she called. "Better be!"

"Yes, Mama," Zora answered, opening the front door. "We just been at the Loving Pine."

I used to eat at home with my mama and daddy every night, just the three of us, except for when my daddy was working out of town. As far back as I can remember, my mama was always out of the house by the time I woke up, gone to work in the laundry at the big Park House hotel in Lake Maitland. A month after my daddy left for Orlando, she picked up a second shift three nights a week. Used to be I had breakfast with my daddy, lunch at school, and supper with my mama and daddy both, but with him gone and her working so much, it was awfully lonely eating. I guess Zora told her mama about it, because the next thing I knew there was Mrs. Hurston visiting my mama, asking if she could spare me the nights she worked late, on account of Mrs. Hurston had so much housework, what with the new baby, and she could really use an extra set of hands.

As we walked into the kitchen, we saw Billie Bronson standing by the sink with Mrs. Hurston. Billie was maybe only twice our age, but she seemed very grown to me — not old so much as earnest. I supposed doing something as important as delivering babies made her very serious about life.

"Hello, Miss Billie," Zora and I said in unison.

"Hey, you two." She had a soft voice, not crackly

like Old Lady Bronson's. Her hands were deep in her apron pockets, but her fingers couldn't keep still. Billie gave Mrs. Hurston a worried glance.

Billie said, "When I left my granny after lunch, she was going to fish some supper and look for some eucalyptus to boil with lavender to help soft up Mrs. Calhoun's back some. Y'all know Mrs. Calhoun's expecting a baby next month?" We nodded, though it was still hard for us to imagine our teacher having a life outside of school. "Well, my granny should have been home hours ago, and I been looking everywhere!"

I had never heard Old Lady Bronson referred to as anyone's grandma before, and the title coupled with the affection in Miss Billie's voice startled me. Realizing that Miss Billie loved Old Lady Bronson made the woman more human to me, even vulnerable. Mrs. Hurston put a reassuring hand on Billie's shoulder and asked us, "Y'all seen Old Lady Bronson around today?"

"We seen her!" Our heads were nodding like leaves in a storm. "We seen her!"

Miss Billie's eyes jumped. "Where? Where did you see her?"

"Over by Blue Sink, fishing!" Zora said. "We were gonna go swimming, but she shooed us away."

"How long ago?"

The time between school letting out and us coming in to help make dinner always seemed to us like most of our waking hours, even though it couldn't have been more than three or four at the most.

"Um, two hours?" It was as good a guess as any.

The crease in Miss Billie's brow came back as she started for the door.

Zora grabbed my hand, and we headed out after Miss Billie.

"Mama," Zora called, "we'll walk with Miss Billie to the Blue Sink and come right back."

We caught up with Miss Billie and fast-walked in silence. I couldn't stop thinking about Mr. Pendir with a gator head instead of his own.

Right before we turned off the road, we saw Mr. Calhoun striding toward us on his way home from the schoolhouse.

"Mr. Calhoun," Miss Billie called, "can you help us look for my grandma?"

Zora sprinted up to Mr. Calhoun. "Old Lady Bronson was late coming home after getting your wife her salve," she blurted out to catch him up. Mr. Calhoun didn't ask any questions, just fell into a quick pace beside us.

There was an eerie stillness at the pond.

"Granny," Miss Billie called out. "Granny, you here?" Her call was met with silence. Mr. Calhoun wiped his forehead with a handkerchief and walked around the west side of the sink. Zora cocked her head, like a forest animal listening for breaking twigs, then darted to the red cliff below where we'd spied the old lady after school. I followed close behind. "Miss Billie, Mr. Calhoun! She's here!" I called. Miss Billie and Mr. Calhoun sprinted over to us. Just below us and below the ledge, sprawled on the rocks, was Old Lady Bronson. A deep purple bruise ringed her right eye and she moaned softly; her eyes were closed. Her fishing rod was floating in the shallow water beside her. I couldn't imagine how she fell from the perch where we'd left her fishing.

Then Miss Billie climbed down the cliff to the rocks and gently cradled her grandmother's head in her lap.

"Oh, Granny!" she whispered. "You OK?"

Old Lady Bronson opened her eyes for just a second and laughed weakly. "You ain't rid of me yet, Billie Marie Bronson!" And with that she fell faint again.

Mr. Calhoun picked Old Lady Bronson up in

his strong and steady arms and carried her up out of the sink. Thin and small as she seemed with her eyes closed, the old lady still had a formidable presence.

Mr. Calhoun smiled at us. "Don't you girls worry. I think she's gonna be OK." Then he and Billie headed off to Old Lady Bronson's house.

Just as they disappeared from the clearing into the trees, we heard a tiny noise that made us both look up. In the twilight we could see the outline of Mr. Pendir's little house. In the doorway, against a light from inside, we saw the unmistakable silhouette of Mr. Pendir leaning against the jamb. His head was as human as mine, but the sight of him watching us sparked my imagination something powerful. Suddenly Zora's story didn't seem so far-fetched at all. Suddenly I believed he might change shape right there in front of us. I heard a booming beat and then realized it was coming from inside me, as if someone had replaced my eardrums with kettledrums.

Zora took my hand. We backed slowly to the tree line, then tore off running to her house.

CHAPTER SEVEN

I had never run so fast. When we stopped to catch our breath, we were halfway to Zora's house and still clutching hands. Zora put her arm around my shoulder, and we heaved air until we could talk.

"You believe me now, don't you?"

I nodded.

"I saw it. That night at the Blue Sink, I saw Mr. Pendir with a gator snout plain as I see you right now. It can't be no accident that Old Lady Bronson—a woman who's never been sick a day in her life— fainted and fell, and Mr. Pendir only a few hundred yards away!"

Zora had stumbled onto something. I couldn't say what it was, but I felt it squirming in my belly.

Back at Zora's house, Mrs. Hurston was busy fixing supper. She was relieved to hear how we'd found Old Lady Bronson. We never said a word about Mr. Pendir, but me and Zora swapped looks all through the meal and dishes.

After Mrs. Hurston had bathed baby Everett and swaddled him tight, she came out on the porch holding him and found us there.

"Why you two out here not even talking? You have a fight?"

"No'm."

"Well, then—"

In the warming presence of her mother, Zora let loose some of her fears.

"Mama, what do you suppose happened to Old Lady Bronson?"

Mrs. Hurston raised an eyebrow. "Didn't you say she fell?"

Zora shook her head. "No'm. We found her on the rocks under that ledge, but when we left her this afternoon, she sat as firmly as a potted plant. I just don't see how she could have slipped."

"What are you saying, child?"

"Do you think something pushed her?" Zora's voice trembled, and I saw her mother's whole body change to her.

"I reckon not. She's a tough bird—besides, there's not a soul in Eatonville would dare to harm a hair on her head!"

"Oh, Mama—" Zora stopped herself for the shortest instant, then she looked her mother square in the eye. "You know about Ghost?"

Mrs. Hurston made a face like Zora had just spoken to her in Seminole. "Say what, now? What ghost is this?"

"Ghost the gator, Mama—the one that killed poor Sonny Wrapped and then disappeared. Just disappeared!"

"Oh, *that* Ghost." Mrs. Hurston sat down between us on the porch step and pulled Zora to her. "That was a terrible thing. Poor foolish boy." She shook her head.

"But Mama, how could Ghost just up and disappear, big as he is? He's the size of three of Daddy laid end to end, yet nobody can find him! It don't make sense unless . . ."

Mrs. Hurston's eyes hooded. "Unless . . . ?"

Zora shifted, unsure how far she could go. "Well,

what if Ghost could turn into a man? Or a man into Ghost? Then nobody would know. . . ."

Mrs. Hurston turned to me. "Carrie, you think men and gators turning into each other, too?"

I looked at my friend, who was nestled against her mama's shoulder, and shrugged. I don't know what kind of face I had on, but I guess it was the kind that made Mrs. Hurston pull me in under her other arm, while her knees kept baby Everett rocking gently in her lap.

"Listen up, both y'all. I never seen a gator turned man, or a man turned gator, or any such thing, in my whole life. I never even heard of one till now, but I'll tell you what: gators is bad enough, and if you ever see one, either of you, you go straight up the first tree you can find, hear? Don't never think you can outrun a gator, but you can sure outclimb one!" She pulled us in tight. "Honestly, you girls!" She chuckled, and it was hard for me not to smile, too.

But Zora stayed serious. "You know Mr. Pendir, Mama?"

The baby started fussing, and Mrs. Hurston picked him up to cradle. "I know him to say hello. Your father says he's a fine carpenter but works too slow. He's not the friendliest squirrel in the nest, but he does his work and minds his business."

When the baby settled, Mrs. Hurston cocked her head. "Why? What about Mr. Pendir?"

Zora looked off at the moon. "Oh, no reason. Just wondering." But she kept frowning.

"What's the matter, baby?" Mrs. Hurston asked. "You still fretting about gators?"

"No, Mama. I just got to thinking of Miss Billie and Old Lady Bronson. Will you promise never to go to the Blue Sink by yourself?"

Mrs. Hurston smiled. "I'm gonna tell you something, Miss Zora Neale. First of all, you know I can't swim and I don't like fishing, so I don't know why I would ever want to go to Blue Sink. Second of all, when is the last time you ever saw me alone?" She nodded toward baby Everett, who stirred in her arms as if on cue. "And finally, if I ever come up missing, it'll be 'cause I turned on my heels with something real important to do. And if that real important thing ever came up, you know I'd be mighty obliged to take you with me."

"You would, Mama? Really?"

"'Course I would. You the only one around this

house that moves in step with me." She glanced at Everett, who was starting to fuss himself awake again.

"Oh, Mama." Zora smiled and wrapped her arms around her mother's neck.

"Oh, Zora Neale." She touched her forehead to her daughter's. "Now, both of you come inside and get some studying done before Carrie has to go home. I'm gonna try to put Everett to bed before he thinks it's time for another feeding."

At that moment, Everett let out a full-on wail, and Mrs. Hurston began to dandle him like he was in a buggy on a bad road. "Oh, Lord, this baby just wake up because I went and mentioned food!"

Zora and I quizzed each other on our multiplication tables and took turns spelling the names of all forty-five states, but Zora had to keep reminding me when it was my turn. All I could think of was how I wanted to run home and hug my own mama as hard as I could.

CHAPTER EIGHT

Zora had to go to Joe Clarke's store after school the next day to pick up some flour and sugar for her mother, so we walked Teddy home, even though it was hardly the most direct route. Zora and I always liked going to the farm.

Before they were our age, Teddy's older brothers Jake and Micah had been pulled out of school for good, to work the farm. By the time Teddy and us were in school, the farm was thriving, and Teddy's parents decided to give their youngest son the chance none of the rest of them had gotten. Teddy was lucky, and he knew it. I don't know if that's why Teddy tried so hard in school and did so well, but I never got the sense that his brothers resented his good luck. If anything, they seemed extra proud of him—but not so proud that they didn't love to tease him.

When we got there, Jake and Micah were hoisting bales of cured tobacco leaves onto the wagon.

"Oh, nice of you to get home just in time for us to be finished with the hard work!" Micah elbowed Jake in the ribs.

"And look," said Jake. "He's brought his two little lady friends with him." Jake pretended to doff a hat he wasn't wearing. "How y'all doing today, ladies?"

"Fine," we said, laughing despite ourselves.

Micah put his arm around Teddy's shoulder, like a minister giving advice to a wayward boy. "Now, brother, how many times do we have to tell you that the law don't like a man to marry two women?"

Jake looked up from pulling the straps tight on the mule's bridle. "It ain't fittin'!"

"That's right," said Micah. "It ain't fittin'!" And as he saw Teddy's mama come out from the farmhouse, he added, for her benefit, "Besides, one woman ought to be more than enough. Look how much trouble Daddy has with Mama—she don't never do what he wants her to do, 'less she wanted to do it herself already!"

Zora and I tried to keep our giggles to ourselves, but we didn't have to worry, because Jake and Micah were howling with laughter. Even Mrs. Baker was smirking a little herself.

"If y'all quit ham-bonin' around and get going," she said, "we might get that tobacco to Lake Maitland in time for the train. Meantime, neither of y'all has to worry about getting married until you find a girl who can get you in a harness next to that mule where you belong—and then let's hope she can tell you apart!"

Everybody laughed at that, Micah and Jake included. It was one of the things I liked so much about Teddy's family—they liked each other's company. They kidded each other, but never to hurt—if the kidding didn't amuse the one being kidded, that would mean they'd gotten it wrong, but I never saw that happen.

After Mrs. Baker sent Jake and Micah on their way, she brought Zora, Teddy, and me into the kitchen and gave us each a thick slice of bread, still warm from the oven, smeared with creamy butter made from their own cows' milk. In the time it took us to eat, she grilled us all on what we were doing in school, what was coming up, how we were going to study, if we were going to go to high school, like Teddy was, and so on. It was nice; it reminded us that school had a purpose beyond the day-to-day, even if we didn't know yet where it would take us. And when we were done, she sent us on our way—"So you can do your chores, and Teddy can do his, and y'all still have time to do your studying after supper."

We all grinned at that. Zora loved to read so much, it hardly felt like studying to her. Unlike me and Teddy, who had to work real hard to stay at the top of the class with her.

My chore for the afternoon was accompanying Zora to Joe Clarke's. Mrs. Hurston might have sent a list with Zora, but Zora was interested in too many other things to be sure to get every item on it, and that's where I came in. I did all the pulling down from shelves, while Zora poked her ears and dipped her mind into grown folks' business—then shared everything she learned with me.

Besides groceries and general items, Joe Clarke's store had more than its share of tall tales and greasy talk. The aisles might have been lined with household goods, but the air was full of the kind of ideas and words respectable ladies wouldn't dare let in their houses—not in the light of day, anyway. So Zora sucked all that adult life right up, smiling, giggling, and listening hard the whole time. I couldn't help but give her sideways looks. Tall talk wasn't for me. But I knew it was part of why Eatonville thrived. We lived in a community without strangers. And the men's stories always felt like the next installment of a good serial.

The usual group of menfolk was on the porch when we came skipping up the walk, and they talked loud as usual, whooping and hollering in a major key. Joe Clarke stood against a post looking right as rain. His marshal badge gleamed in the sunlight, and his pistol sat on his hip.

"Why, hello, Carrie," Mr. Clarke said. "And hello, Zora."

We helloed him back, somewhere between polite and shy. Joe Clarke was a big man, but it wasn't his bigness that made us a little shy. Zora's father was just as tall. But I always believed that Joe Clarke was not only the strongest and bravest man in town, but the smartest; after my father, he was also the gentlest and the kindest.

"It's been heard all around town this day that you

two are mighty deserving children, Miss Zora Neale Hurston and Miss Carrie Brown," Mr. Clarke said. "Mighty deserving." He poked out his already protruding belly, and he snapped his red suspenders. The gold chain of his pocket watch swayed on the hip opposite his pistol.

"Mighty deserving? What for? We didn't win any spelling bee." Zora smiled. "Not yet, anyway." She gave me a wink. She prided herself on knowing more words than anybody in the school—teachers possibly included—and knowing how to spell them to boot, but she never talked fancy without a good reason.

"Girls, y'all been pegged for doing something a whole lot more important than spelling some words out. If it wasn't for you two, Old Lady Bronson might still be lying where she fell down at Blue Sink."

Zora looked up at Joe Clarke. "You believe she fell, Mr. Clarke?"

Joe Clarke's eyebrows rose quizzically. "Well, way I heard it, she had a little fainting spell. . . ." It obviously hadn't occurred to him to question the story.

"Old Lady Bronson tell you that?" I didn't know what Zora was thinking, but I could see the gears spinning.

"Why, no, it was Mr. Calhoun told me. But—"

One of the men on the porch interrupted him. "Hey, Marshal—I didn't know you hired yourself a deputy!" That brought a round of chuckles, but I could tell they were curious just the same. Zora, though, didn't have a speck of laughing in her. Joe Clarke saw that, and I watched him put his own smile in his pocket as he sat down on a little end of the bench to face Zora eye to eye.

"Let's see, now. Dave Calhoun come in real early this morning with a cracked shoe on the right front of that paint mule of his. He said Old Lady Bronson was fishing at Blue Sink yesterday and had a fainting spell—"

He put his hand up to hold off any protest Zora might have made. "I'm just telling what I heard! He said she likely had a fainting spell on that little ledge that comes out, and fell straight over onto the rocks, and that's where y'all found her. Said another couple of feet and she would have landed in the water and drowned for sure. She was banged up real good as it was," he said. "But the whole thing I'm trying to say, the whole reason I brought this up, is that Old Lady Bronson would probably still be there if it hadn't been for you!"

Now he allowed himself a smile, but Zora didn't.

She drew herself up, like she was about to recite for class, and said, "Mr. Clarke, I don't think Old Lady Bronson fainted or even just slipped."

There was some noise from the porch, but Mr. Clarke waved his hand like a preacher asking for a moment of silence. "You don't? What you think, then?"

"No, sir. I think a gator knocked her onto those rocks with his tail. That's what I think. I warned her, too. Carrie was there—she'll tell you."

I said, "That's right," but Zora was still talking, so I don't think anybody heard me.

"I even told my mama about it. Since you the marshal, I guess I should have told you." Zora took a deep breath. "I saw Mr. Pendir turn into a gator with my own two eyes. I was out at the Blue Sink night before last, and I saw Mr. Pendir standing on his porch with a gator snout instead of a head!"

For an instant I had a feeling that the whole porch was about to explode laughing. But no—aside from a single snort and a tongue click, there was just a bunch of grins. The porch didn't take Zora's accusations about Mr. Pendir seriously, but they understood that *we* were serious. Joe Clarke understood best of all.

"Now, Zora. I'm gone tell you something and I

want you to listen very good. You too, Carrie. You both listening?"

"Yes, sir," Zora said. "I'm listening."

I bobbed my head.

"It ain't nice to say things like that about folks. Especially old, lonely folks. Pendir — he don't have no place on that wrinkled face to hide a thing like being something other than what he is. Y'all understand? Most folks only got so many hiding places. And I'm afraid old Pendir's face ain't one of his."

"Well, what is my face telling you, Mr. Clarke?" Zora was fearless. And sometimes her courage was so bold it spilled onto me and pushed away my fear, for at least a second.

Joe Clarke got eye level with us. "I see what's called a Zora on your face." She beamed like the sun had an extra ray just for her. "And what's on yours," he said to me, "is something called Carrie." I got my own ray, too.

"What you see is Zora," Zora repeated slowly, as if she were hearing her own name for the first time.

"That's right, girl. And Zora saved that old lady just the same as if Zora picked her up off those rocks and carried her home herself."

"She did?"

Joe Clarke smiled. "She did."

Mr. Eddie Jackson, a short, skinny man with nutmeg skin, tipped his hat at us. "Good job."

A thin, greasy-haired man named Mr. Slayton asked, "What the grown men to do around these parts if little girls gone be the ones saving folks?"

"What the grown men got to do then," Joe Clarke said, "is give the little girls as much licorice as they can eat." He opened the screen door of his store for us, went behind the counter, and pulled out a nearly full box of licorice sticks.

"Ladies, have as many as you like."

We had no shame. Zora began to fill the pockets of her shift with the sweet twisty whips. I followed suit, and when we got through with cramming our dress pockets, we put as many of the sticks as we could on the inside of our knee socks, stuffing what didn't fit there into our shoes. Zora tried walking a few steps and found that she couldn't — not so much because her feet hurt as because walking threw too much of the candy clear out of her shoes. So she took off her bucks and filled them with the licorice, too, like little Easter baskets.

"More room without my feet," she said.

"You want your licorice sticks tasting like feet?" I asked.

Mr. Clarke laughed like a good-natured giant.

"Shucks, I don't hardly wear my shoes no way," Zora answered.

Stumped for an answer to that, I sucked on a licorice stick.

Just then Chester Cools rode up to the store on his sad old mule. "An awful thing happened, Joe," Mr. Cools muttered. "Awful thing!"

CHAPTER NINE

There's a body by the tracks!" Chester sputtered. "It don't have no head. The body don't have no head. . . ."

The whole porch gasped, then fell quiet. Goose pimples sprung up all over my body, like I had been dipped in ice-cold water. Zora was almost twitching. She turned to me to make a silent *Shh!* sign, her eyes hot with interest.

Chester Cools had a small farm not far from the railroad tracks that ran from Jacksonville to Lake Maitland and shot along the edge of Eatonville. We inched closer to the screen door to hear, but no one noticed.

"What you say?" Joe Clarke said in disbelief.

"I said, they a dead man by the tracks! Y'all deaf?"

"Who—who is it?" a quivering voice from the porch chorus asked.

Mr. Cools was shaking. "How am I supposed to know? The man's head is gone. His head is gone!"

Another voice: "That leave me out! I still got my head."

There was nervous laughter, but Joe Clarke waved his hand and the menfolk shushed up. He put his hand on Mr. Cools's shoulder.

"Pay 'em no mind, Chester. Folks forget how to act when they can't stand a truth."

Mr. Cools shot a look at the men, who were all long faces now, solemn as a jury.

Joe Clarke went on. "Anything special about him?"

Mr. Cools closed his eyes and tilted his head back, making a mental catalog of the man. "Mm, nothing special. Wearing overalls, beat-up boots. Probably a turpentine worker in Lake Maitland . . ." He blinked. "Huh—had a braided red strap on his shoulder."

"Was there . . . ?" Joe Clarke started to ask a question and then stopped, like he was afraid to ask the rest.

Mr. Cools lit up a little suddenly, remembering more. "Hey, did I say about the git-tar? They was a git-tar few feet away. All smashed to pieces, though—can't do nothing with it."

"Oh, sweet Lord!" Joe Clarke barely whispered the words: "Oh, sweet Lord!"

"What is it, Joe?" another anonymous voice asked. Mr. Clarke didn't answer. He turned his back on the men and put one hand on the screen door, hanging his head down low. Zora and I were still on the other side of the screen, but he never saw us, and we didn't make a sound.

"Take me there," Joe Clarke said to Chester. "Now."

Mr. Cools got back on his mule, Joe swung up on his pretty bay mare, and they went off. Half the men on the porch trailed them on foot. The other half went their own ways. Zora and me were left alone.

"We knew him," Zora said. "The man without a head. We knew him."

I was looking at the floor but I couldn't see it right. Then I was sitting down. And Zora was sitting next to me with her arm around my shoulder. I shook my head.

"Yes, we did," she said in a soft voice that almost

didn't sound like her. "We did, Carrie. I'm sorry, girl, but we did."

I don't know when it sank in and I started sobbing. It seemed like a long time before I stopped. I couldn't think why I was so broken up about a man I had met just the day before, a man who sang a little and chatted with us a little and was gone inside half an hour. Ivory was just a traveling worker with a sweet voice. But he was dead, and he wasn't coming back. I kept sobbing, and Zora kept saying, "I know, I know."

Finally I stood and wiped my eyes and swallowed hard. "Who would do that? And why would somebody do that to a man? Why?"

Something moved across Zora's face, an idea that started just under her bottom lip and rode up to her eyebrows.

"You remember what Ivory said?" She cocked her head and gave me a long, penetrating look. "That he was going to go swimming in the Blue Sink last night!"

A shiver ran down my spine. "But Zora," I said, "that doesn't mean it was Mr. Pendir who killed him!"

Even as I said it, I didn't believe my own doubting. And my asking seemed to make Zora surer of her own judgment.

"Ain't no regular folks do nothing like we just heard, Carrie. It's not a somebody that cuts off and steals a man's head—it's a some*thing*."

Only a monster could do what was done to Ivory.

CHAPTER TEN

We had only known about Ivory's death for a few hours when it came suppertime in the Hurston household. The news had spread through Lake Maitland and Eatonville, and a pall had already fallen on the whole town.

Like many a traveling man, Mr. Hurston wanted nothing to dampen his spirits before a trip, and so he determined not to let the evil of the world spoil his last night with his family before leaving to preach in Orlando for a week.

Mr. Hurston had been home only two weeks since his last trip, and to make up for another absence so soon, he promised each one of the Hurston boys and girls a gift of their choosing from the big town. Sitting around the dinner table that night after a good filling meal of hoecake and collards, it felt like the sun was shining indoors. Pitchers of fresh-squeezed lemonade rushed down our throats.

Sarah went first. She was far and away her father's favorite, but she never rubbed it in. She didn't have to. I had known the Hurstons my entire life. During that time I had never seen Sarah with a trailing hem, a hair out of place, or a grass-stained dress, and I learned from watching her that a daddy's girl isn't a kind of person, but a species. Neither Zora nor I belonged to it.

"I want some lace, Daddy, to trim my recital dress with." Sarah was the only one who was allowed music lessons proper. In fact, Mr. Hurston had bought a piano for Sarah alone.

Mr. Hurston beamed with pride. "What color you want, honey?" Sarah, prim and proper, beamed back.

"Pink and white, Daddy," Sarah cooed.

"Then, darling, that's what you'll get."

And so went the ritual. John wanted a chemistry book—"Anything about chemistry!" Joel pleaded his case for multicolored jacks. Even the baby of the family, Everett, sitting on his mother's lap, knew when it was his turn. He couldn't make words yet, but he made enough sounds to get his point across.

"I think my baby boy is telling me he wants a new rattle!" Mr. Hurston laughed, and the rest of the table laughed with him; Everett laughed too, and that made his father roar. Satisfaction was still in the air, and Mr. Hurston was sucking it up in gulps. Then it was Zora's turn.

"Daddy, I don't care about a gift," she said. "I want to talk about the man they found by the tracks. . . ."

As soon as the words left Zora's mouth, you could see the good feeling flee the room. We froze in our seats. Mr. Hurston gripped the arms of his chair and pushed slowly back from the head of the table, his eyes fixed on Zora. Baby Everett looked up at his mother, but even he didn't make a peep. Mrs. Hurston looked at her husband as if her eyes alone could temper him. They couldn't. Her understanding of Zora's curiosity and conviction was no match for Mr. Hurston's sudden rage. Before Zora could continue her story, her father stood and placed his palms flat against the table.

"Girl," he said with a roll of thunder on his tongue, "we will not talk about such things at my table!" Some people feel a child should not speak unless spoken to. Mr. Hurston didn't mind if children talked, so long as we didn't say anything he didn't want to hear. That meant the questions children ask when something terrible happens were especially out of bounds.

Zora was a slow student of that school on the best of days. She blinked hopefully. "But Daddy, I think I know what killed him, and we got to do something. We just got to!" I wanted to slide under the table and hide till the storm passed.

"Do you — do you think you *white?*" Mr. Hurston was shaking with anger. His face was twitching. "Wanting to talk about death — right here at the dinner table! That is the kind of thing white folks do!"

"Everyone at this table knows who they are," Mrs. Hurston interrupted quietly.

"I beg to differ, Lucy. I beg to differ. But this ain't between me and you. It's between me and this child."

Zora stood up slowly, slid her chair under the table, and stood behind it. I could see it took all the courage she had. "Saying what I know and wanting answers," she said, "doesn't make me white. I know who I am. I'm Zora."

Of all the Hurston children, Zora looked the most like her father, and I think the likeness only fueled his anger. Sometimes there's nothing more aggravating than looking in a mirror.

From what Mrs. Hurston told us, her husband had been glad to open his heart and home to his third child—and first daughter—when Sarah was born. He just never counted on having to do it a second time. The one thing in John Hurston's life that had truly surprised him was Zora being born a girl. He often said that he couldn't forgive Zora for playing such a trick on him. Just by being born she had proven that not even the affairs of his own home were totally under his control. And if there was one thing Mr. Hurston didn't like, it was being shown up.

"Sit, Zora." Mrs. Hurston spoke in a calm, low voice. "Sit down, child."

Zora hated to disobey her mother. But she set her lips and shook her head, never meeting her mother's gaze. She didn't have it in her to swallow shame when she felt wronged.

"Oh, I see," Mr. Hurston said, an angry smile playing on his lips. "You telling me who you are now. Well, let me tell you something. If it wasn't for me, there wouldn't be a Zora. And if it's up to me, there won't be a Zora much longer!"

Mr. Hurston took two strides the length of the

table, arriving in front of Zora like a wraith carried on the wind. He raised his hand to strike her. Zora gripped the back of her chair, but didn't flinch.

Suddenly Mrs. Hurston cried out—called her husband's name. That one sound, that one syllable, was a brick wall shielding her daughter's face from her husband's hand.

I can't count the times I saw Mr. Hurston's love of his wife spare Zora physical pain. But he never spared Zora other kinds of hurt.

"Do you know what being white is? Being white is wanting things that are out of your reach. And for white folks, that's fine and dandy, 'cause they stand niggers one on top of the other to pull down from the sky what they want. But you don't got no ladder, Zora." Zora jerked her head back—his words fell on her like a blow.

"That's enough," Lucy Hurston said.

"That child of yours don't got sense," Mr. Hurston chided. "Ruining my last night at home with talk of a murder! She ain't mine. She's all yours, Lucy. All yours."

"Then let what's mine be." Mrs. Hurston stood with Everett in one arm, taking an empty pitcher in the other. All of the Hurston children except Zora took their mother's cue and began to clear the table. Mr. Hurston continued to stand, staring at Zora, empty-handed and silent; then he shook his head, turned, and strode into the parlor.

Zora sulked away toward the front door, and I followed her. She turned around and looked at me when we got to the gardenia bushes.

"I don't feel much like talking, Carrie." There was a quiver in her voice.

"All righty," I responded. "You'll feel better if I don't say anything. So that's what I'm going to do: stand here beside you without saying a word."

Zora tried to smile, but she couldn't manage it and leash her tears, too. So she made a face somewhere between getting a cramp in your foot and a gnat in your eye.

We sat for a half hour or so, not talking, just smelling the gardenia and listening to the cicada sing.

Walking home later, I thought about the difference between a mama's girl and a daddy's girl. I decided that a daughter who belongs to her daddy expects gifts, while a daughter who belongs to her mama expects a lot more. Not from her mama. From herself.

CHAPTER ELEVEN

E ven though I felt sad about Zora's troubles with her father, I would have welcomed some trouble with mine. The thing about not seeing someone for a long time, especially someone that you love, is that your memory of them becomes one-sided. Or at least that's what happened to me.

Except for him leaving, all of my memories of my daddy were good ones. Him fixing me breakfast because my mama had to leave so early. Him singing "Sleep, Little Pretty One" to me when I woke up crying from a bad dream. Him carrying me to bed after I fell asleep on the front step watching fireflies buzz by like shooting stars. Him laughing and the flash of his smile when he tickled my feet and saw — I hope — joy mixed up with love all over my face. I had a collection of those memories that I used to sift through before I went to sleep, making sure I remembered every detail of each one, even straining to find another detail I might have missed so I could add it to the treasure.

My favorite thing to chew on from the treasure box was the singing. Maybe it was because my eyes had always been closed when he sang to me that it was easy for me to pretend to myself that he was still right there. He never sang the blues — mostly hymns and lullabies and songs he just made up — but suddenly I felt like I was remembering that he did. I could even hear his voice.

But good things alone don't make up a person who's real. For someone to be real in my heart and my head, I have to take the good about them with the bad. I knew my father used to do things that bothered me, or make me do chores I didn't feel like doing, but one day I realized I just couldn't remember them. I think he didn't like me to track mud in from outside . . . but that's all I could think of. That's when I knew he wasn't real to me anymore, that he had been gone too long—when the things that got on my nerves about him faded from my memory.

Not for my mama, though. She was different. I always knew when she thought about my father, good parts and bad, because she would clean up our little house even when it didn't need it—when our three tiny rooms couldn't stand another scrubbing. What Mama couldn't put away in her heart, she always found a place for in a drawer or a cupboard.

Saturdays, my mama's cleaning was at its most fevered. It was the only day she didn't work or go to church. It was a time devoted to absence—my father's, and dirt's. But not even cleaning could ruin my Saturday morning, because it was the only day of the week I didn't have to wake up and be somewhere straightaway. I never minded school, and church always felt like what church should be. It was just that being with my own mama in our own little home for a day held a special magic for me. Bleach and soap and starch, ironed clothes and piney floors, all smell like Mama to me, even to this day.

By the early afternoon, the cleaning was all done, and I was sitting with my mama on the front step. She was resting after hanging out the wash to dry, and I was tucked up under her arm, soaking up the fact that she was sitting still at all. Then right when Mama stood up to finish chores, the creaking in her back loud as a rusty hinge, Zora and Mrs. Hurston strolled up.

After what had happened at supper the night before, I didn't know when I might see Zora again. So seeing her right then was an unexpected treat. Mama seemed surprised, too.

"Etta," said Mrs. Hurston, "I'm sorry for just showing up on a Saturday like this when I know you got things to tend, but I was wondering if I could take Carrie with me and Zora over to Lake Maitland. Sarah's home practicing piano for church and minding the baby, and we have some guests coming next week I got to buy some towels for. And our girls should have some kind of fun that don't need staining up their clothes something awful."

I looked at my mama real hard while Mrs. Hurston stated her case. She didn't have Mama until she mentioned stained clothes. If Mama hadn't just finished laundry, I don't think I would have been allowed to go. Mama's knuckles were still raw from the steaming water. She looked at her hands before she spoke.

"You know, Lucy, I ain't never thought of that

before. If Carrie here became a little more ladylike, I'd have less trouble scrubbing clothes. Indeed you can take my girl with you. She need a little civilizing."

"Same here for this one." Mrs. Hurston smiled at Zora, who was nearly her mother's height. "Same here."

Zora and I held Mrs. Hurston's hands the whole way to Lake Maitland, just the three of us. I figured our trip was like a bandage on the wound Mr. Hurston had delivered to Zora the previous night. During our walk, Mrs. Hurston kept asking, "How y'all feeling?" Without fail, both of us responded, "Fine." But I could tell Zora wasn't fine so much as better. And Mrs. Hurston knew that the fastest way to heal Zora was for her to spend time with people she loved. That afternoon I was a patch on a healing blanket.

CHAPTER TWELVE

The town of Lake Maitland was a pretty busy place, even back then. Between the pine forests and the orange groves and the packing house and the ice factory and the stables, there was thousands of people living and working there — half the people in Eatonville went there for work, like my mama. It was a fancy place, too, maybe not as swanky as Winter Park, but folks from cold places all over — even presidents! — thought it was worth the trip to spend the winter in Lake Maitland.

This particular Saturday, the town was crawling with folks who cared about more things than I could count. A great many of them were concerned with looking sharp as tacks. Others couldn't see what was right in front of them for how busy they were trying to get where they were going. The sun was hot, but that was the least of Lake Maitland's heat. The rattle of wagon wheels, the hollow clatter of horseshoes, and the rumble of an occasional automobile engine created a warmth on the ground that might as well have been baking our feet. We hopped and skipped like coal embers were grazing our toes right through our shoes. When we ran into Mrs. Eunice Jefferson in the linen store, she also seemed jumpy, but in a different way. She had springs in her jaws.

Mrs. Jefferson was in the back of the store where the towels were stacked. The shop was lovely and cool. Fabric for bed sheets was on big spools in the store window. Beaded pillows trimmed with all colors of lace lined the shelves. Some were velvet. Others were silk. I wanted to touch my face to each one. I wanted to rub luxury on my skin, and I wanted a little luxury to rub off on me. I didn't know otherwise how to take any home to my mama.

Zora wasn't nearly as interested in what I considered to be the store's treasures as she was in sticking her nose in grown folks' business.

"A murder in Eatonville got the white folks over here awful nervous," Mrs. Jefferson whispered. "I know what gets under they skin better than most. Being in someone's house, cleaning up they slop, you can't help but get they thoughts rubbed off on you. No matter how down deep they think they got 'em locked up, either. If there's one person it's hard to hide a thought from, it sure is a maid."

"That ain't no kind of talk for children," Mrs. Hurston whispered back, but Mrs. Jefferson must not have heard her, because she just kept on.

"'Course white folks don't care who it was. Not that anybody know—he wasn't kin to anybody in these parts or we'd have heard by now. Probably one of them turpentine workers riding a freight train and fell off, like a fool." Mrs. Jefferson clucked.

Mrs. Hurston leaned over and shooed us out. "Wait for me outside, you two."

"But that ain't none of my business," we heard Mrs. Jefferson say, and she started in on another topic. "Now, if you want to hear something . . ."

Zora grabbed my hand and pulled me behind a large bale of fabric, where we could go on listening. Zora wasn't about to let any grown folks' talk slip through her fingers.

Mrs. Jefferson was off to the races. ". . . call herself Gold. Gold! Now, what kind of a name is that? Who call theyself Gold?" Mrs. Jefferson clicked her tongue—or maybe it was Mrs. Hurston. "But that ain't the best part. You know white folks can't see like we do," Mrs. Jefferson said. "You had to *see* this girl! If you would have seen her, Lucy, you couldn't have missed her."

"Is she that pretty?"

"I guess some folks would say she is. Now the stack of new tablecloths she left here with," Mrs. Jefferson whispered, "*they* sure was pretty!"

Mrs. Jefferson didn't stop there.

"But that ain't the best part! Just yesterday, I was at the butcher for the Jones's Sunday dinner when Gold done traipsed her way in proud as she want to be. Lucy, this girl done had a white man accompany her to the butcher! But that ain't the best part!"

"Then what is?" Mrs. Hurston asked, her words bubbling with curious, amused laughter.

There was a pause. I guessed that Mrs. Jefferson was looking over her shoulder. Then she spoke in the loudest whisper I ever heard: "Her and the white man engaged to get *married!*"

Mrs. Hurston gasped. And Zora had finally had

her fill of silence and invisibility. She popped up from behind the bale like a weasel. "What y'all talking about? Who's getting married?"

Suddenly the fun was over.

"What are y'all doing here?" Mrs. Hurston was more irritated than angry. "Didn't I tell you both to wait for me outside?" Zora didn't have a chance to answer. The owner of the store, a white woman named Mrs. Walcott, suddenly appeared from behind the counter.

"What's all this ruckus?" Her voice was sharp.

"Just children, ma'am. Just children," Mrs. Jefferson answered. "I'm done with Mrs. Jones's picking out for the afternoon. These dish towels will be all."

Mrs. Walcott also eyed the two ivory towels draped over Mrs. Hurston's arm. They looked the same to me as clouds. The way the white woman stared at them, they might as well have been.

"What are those towels for?"

Mrs. Hurston didn't hesitate. "I've started doing some housework for some folks here in town. They're having guests arrive tomorrow. These are for them."

Zora got a strange look in her eye, but she knew better than to blurt out the truth, as her mother told the kind of lie we'd all heard plenty of times before.

79

Eatonville's motto might as well have been: no need for white folks to know our business; best to let them think they got the upper hand.

Since folks always called these kinds of answers "white lies," Zora and I reckoned it was because white folks required lies from us. That's not to say that we thought of our business, our lives, as particularly colored or Negro. We just didn't think white people needed to be privy to everything that was ours. Our lives and our selves weren't simply anyone's for the taking.

"Well, I'll ring it all up now," Mrs. Walcott said, satisfied, and took both sets of towels to the register. Mrs. Jefferson and Mrs. Hurston followed behind her, and we followed behind them. We were all silent.

When we got outside, I looked at the two women holding their packages—Mrs. Jefferson's for her employer, and Mrs. Hurston's for her own household—and I couldn't see any difference between the two women. It picked at my spirit that the surest way for Negroes to get along was to pretend we were only ever running errands for white folks. Didn't people like Mrs. Walcott think anything belonged to us?

But a different lie suddenly took center stage.

CHAPTER THIRTEEN

The first time I saw Gold, I realized there's no such thing as good-looking people or bad-looking people. There's just people you see and people you don't.

Folks couldn't help but see Gold. They couldn't take their eyes off her. She was the sun.

Mrs. Jefferson and us were saying our good-byes in front of the linen store when Gold appeared arm in arm with her man. She wore a beautiful flower-print dress, fancier than Sunday clothes but worn with an easy grace that said she didn't think the dress was special. She held a matching parasol and walked with a light music in her step. She might have been a spirit.

She seemed more beautiful than any living person I had ever seen.

Mrs. Hurston and Mrs. Jefferson stopped dead in their tracks. But they didn't eye Gold nearly as carefully as they did the man she was with. I don't know why. Next to her, he wasn't much to look at.

The man was tall as Joe Clarke, and walked with his chest poked out. He was sweaty. Stains darkened both sides of his white morning coat from the armpits almost to his waist. I wasn't surprised, either. It could have been the flame in Gold's shining brown eyes that got him running water so.

I had never seen anything like Gold. Her face was round and soft. Her hair was blond and fell around her face in loose waves and midway down her back. Her lips held the shape of a smile. Ease was just her natural expression. And under the entire surface of her peach-fuzz skin there was the glow of candlelight.

Gazing at her, drinking her in, I imagined that if a disagreeable moment had tapped her on the shoulder, Gold wouldn't have recognized it. I couldn't picture a world where her kind of person knew trouble.

A window full of horseshoes got the man's attention, and he wandered off for a closer look. Gold continued walking straight ahead on her own, and now

Mrs. Jefferson and Mrs. Hurston were trying to ignore her. They couldn't. Not only was Gold walking in our direction; she was walking straight toward us. To be exact, I think she was drawn straight to Zora. She must have recognized a familiar light beaming from inside my friend.

"Good afternoon, ladies," she said.

Mrs. Jefferson got full of huffs and puffs, and Mrs. Hurston stood up straighter. Gold spoke respectfully, but she wasn't looking at the older women. Zora and I were her intended audience.

The beautiful lady was talking directly to us. Whatever it was that made her so beautiful must have been inside of us, too. We were pleased as punch, and nervous.

Neither Mrs. Jefferson nor Mrs. Hurston said a word. Their shared expression said it all. They flashed her the fake smiles of caution, of good sense.

"Afternoon! My name is Zora!" Zora's words were bouncier than a ball. "What's yours?"

"It's not polite to ask strangers questions, Zora," Mrs. Hurston interrupted.

"It's quite all right," the woman said. "Hello, Zora. My name is Gold." Then she looked at me. "And what's your name?"

"Carrie. Ma'am." I felt the urge to curtsy, or bow, but I didn't know how to do either one, so I just bobbed my head a second.

"Well, it's a pleasure to meet both of you," Gold said. And a beat later the man came up from behind and grabbed her hand. I didn't know if he was done looking at the horseshoes or not, but he had certainly been in a rush to get to Gold. In only a few feet, he had nearly gotten clear out of breath.

"Why are you talking to . . . these . . . people?" His voice was loud, with a nervous, strained authority. Then his eyes shifted, checking to see if anyone was watching us. Once he established that no one was — too many people streaming past all around us — he tugged firmly at Gold's wrist.

She didn't budge; she stood her ground — sort of. She placed her hand on top of his, as if she took his gesture for affection. "Just a moment, William, dear. I'm saying good-bye to my friends Zora and Carrie." She spoke in the same sugary calm tone, though without looking at him. Then she said, "Bye-bye, ladies," like she had been chatting with old friends and the conversation had come to a natural end. "It was lovely to chat with you. You take care, now."

Zora waved to her, and I did the same. As the

couple walked away, we could hear the man asking
Gold in a fevered whisper, "Who are those people?
How do you know them?" She kept her hand on his
and turned her smile to the opposite side of the street.
I don't know if she answered him.

"Can you believe the nerve of that woman?" Mrs.
Jefferson practically hissed.

"I surely cannot," Mrs. Hurston shot back. "And
that man doesn't want to let her out of his sight. She
best be careful."

"About what?" Zora chimed.

Mrs. Hurston met Zora's eyes. "She best be careful about being too friendly with people she gave up
her place with."

I was puzzled. "Who's that? Who are Gold's
people?"

Mrs. Hurston only answered, "Some folks are too
dangerous to have people."

Mrs. Jefferson sucked her teeth in agreement, then
left us without a word, strolling in what just happened
to be the same direction as Gold and her William.

Mrs. Hurston shook her head. "I suppose Mrs.
Jefferson wants to find out if that ain't the best part."
With the little parcel of towels under her arm, she
took our hands again and resumed our journey, which

I suspected was more about seeing than buying in the first place.

Not much could have had the power to pull Zora's attention away from what we had just seen, but amazingly, moments later we stumbled onto something that did.

Of all the shops on Maitland Avenue, Lake Maitland's main street, it was always the bookseller that drew Zora in like a fish hooked on a line. I wasn't half the reader she was, but today something in the plate-glass window made us both stop. Propped up center stage was a thick green book, its linen cover greener for the black-inked words pressed into its surface: *The Myth and Lore of Gator Country.*

We couldn't believe our eyes. A whole book—a majestic book—consecrated to the monster at the heart of our mystery. Was it a dusty dry cyclopedia of facts? Or was it the answer to our prayers—a book of revelation, a key to secrets? The cover drawing etched in black told us everything: a gator emerging from a curtain of swamp grass was headed right at us, turning its head just a little so we could see its vicious grin.

We pressed our hands and noses against the glass. You could hear us breathe.

Mrs. Hurston had been watching us. I knew it

pleased her that her daughter was moved by books and words, that Zora had eyes to see the world and the wits to express what she saw. So when Zora turned to her mother, Mrs. Hurston already recognized the pleading in her eyes.

"Honey, you know we're blessed in a lot of ways, but we only have just so much money. And that book—" She stared at the paper tag on a string that trailed from the spine. "That book costs more than these towels. I'm sorry."

"I know, Mama," Zora answered, looking down to hide the disappointment in her eyes. "I understand."

Mrs. Hurston tenderly smoothed her daughter's hair and took hold of both our hands for the walk home.

When we got back to the Hurstons' yard, we climbed the chinaberry tree and just sat up there awhile thinking about the book. After that we climbed down and chased each other around the tree until we got dizzy. I plopped down on the ground. Zora plopped down beside me. A monarch butterfly fluttered in our wake, the black outlines on its white-and-bright-orange wings like shards of stained glass.

"You think that butterfly could be a fairy?" Zora asked.

"I don't know."

"I wanna follow it."

"You do?"

"Yeah, I do. Come on, Carrie. You got legs to run on, don't you?"

CHAPTER FOURTEEN

The butterfly danced in the air out of Zora's yard and down the road. It led us about a quarter mile before it decided to take us into the woods.

It was around four in the afternoon. The sky wasn't nearly ready for the sun to set, but everything was lit up just right, like there were chandeliers of candlelight swinging from the top of every tree.

I ran my hand along the glossy pine needles for the tickle. The trees swayed back and forth like they were listening to a choir. The Bermuda grass was singing soft and clear for them.

And the butterfly—it was the star of the show! Flitting up and down and side to side, in long straight lines and cockeyed circles, it was curious about everything and nothing at all. And when we wound up at Blue Sink, where the butterfly had led us, it disappeared in the long shadow of a cypress tree, as if the forest floor had opened its mouth and swallowed the butterfly without even a splash of rainwater to wash it down.

"Hurry! Make a wish!" Zora gasped. "It must have been a fairy."

We silently made our wishes, holding hands on the edge of the cool shadow. I wished that Zora and me would be friends forever. And that instead of tomorrow being Sunday, it would be Saturday all over again.

"Zora," I asked, "what you wish for?" But she didn't have a chance to answer. We had company. It was Mr. Ambrose, the old white man who had helped deliver Zora into the world.

Zora's father used to make most of his money from being a carpenter, and he still made cabinets and such from time to time after he got the call to preach, especially when people who knew his work wanted to pay him well for it. Mr. Ambrose, who had a pretty brick house in Lake Maitland right on Horatio Avenue, was one of those people; the year he built his house, the year Zora and Teddy and I were born, he gave Mr. Hurston one project after another.

It was one day during that year, when Mr. Hurston was away preaching in Osceola and Mrs. Hurston was home alone with the children, that Zora got the idea to come into the world two weeks early. Luckily Mr. Ambrose got the idea to drop by the Hurston house with some fresh pork and vegetables. He arrived minutes after Zora was born—just in time to cut the belly cord. He said the gator bass in her brand-new lungs had called him to that house just the same as if she had been yelling his name. Mr. Ambrose never got tired of telling Zora the story. And Zora never got tired of hearing it.

He liked to say that Blue Sink was his favorite fishing hole. He didn't get there much, but neither of us was surprised to find him there.

"Snidlets," he called, "what you and Carrie doing over there?"

"We just wishing, is all," Zora called back.

Only Mr. Ambrose called her Snidlets. Being there when someone is born makes folks want to name a child. The old man had earned the privilege.

"Then come do some wishing over here by me. The fish are biting, and I don't wanna leave my line."

We marched over to him. He was sitting on the same ledge where we last saw Old Lady Bronson. He and Zora started talking at the exact same time, but she stopped so he could go on. There was kind of an order to the talk, not rules but a little ritual they both observed.

"How your mama and daddy?"

"Good," she said.

"Your daddy still preachin'?"

"Yes, sir, but mostly over in Sanford, so we don't hardly get to hear him, except when he's practicing."

"He doing any woodworking these days?"

"Not too much. Just in the house sometimes."

"Best carpenter in the county."

Zora smiled. "I know it."

"How your big brothers doing?"

"Good. Bob's finishing his first year of medical school up in Nashville, and Ben's been courtin' Johnetta Sims, and keeps going to her daddy's pharmacy just to look at her."

"I reckon someday somebody's gonna be courting you, Snidlets!"

"Oh, no—courtin' just gets folks stuck in one place forever."

He laughed. "The baby—he growin' good?"

She was smiling, like he was building up to a joke and she saw it coming. He was smiling, too. "Yes, sir."

"I feel like I'm forgetting somebody important. Oh, your sister? How's she doin'?"

Zora cut her eyes at him in a way that made him snort. "Mr. Ambrose, she is just sugar and spice and everything nice!"

Now they both laughed, and I did, too. I felt good, watching them—two people knowing what the other one thinks and playing with what they know, not to entertain themselves but to entertain each other.

The little ritual went on for another couple of minutes, Mr. Ambrose asking Zora all about school and what she was learning and how she was doing and telling her what was coming next ("Oh, you gonna love algebra, Snidlets—they made that stuff up just for people who think like you!"), even asking how Teddy was doing, and Teddy's folks, and Teddy's brothers.

Then he turned to me and asked me how *my* mama

was, and how *I* was doing in school, and if I was staying out of trouble and so forth, and I answered as polite as I knew how. I wasn't used to white folks asking me about much of anything at all, much less my real self, so I answered mostly "Good" and "Yes, sir."

Finally, we had passed all the preliminaries and he turned back to Zora. "So, Snidlets. What you two so fired up about? I know it's bound to be something good."

"Oh, it ain't good, but it's definitely something," Zora answered, all the leisure in her voice now gone. "You hear about that man they found by the tracks?"

"I did. What you know about that?"

"His name was Ivory," Zora declared. "We knew him. And we know who killed him and stole his head."

The old man blinked; then he blinked again. "And who would that be, Snidlets?"

"It was the gator man," Zora said. "A man who can turn himself into a gator."

"And how you reckon he does that, exactly?" the old man asked, the gruffness of his voice rimming with interest.

"Me and Carrie here could find out how, if we only had this book we saw in Lake Maitland today."

Then Zora took a big breath and told the story of how we were there when Ghost got Sonny Wrapped, and how that big gator up and vanished after that. "Folks searched for weeks, but they couldn't find a trace!"

Then she told him about Old Lady Bronson. "You hear about Old Lady Bronson falling onto those rocks down there? Well, I don't think she had no accident. The gator man most likely swatted her with his tail and knocked her down. And Ivory, that man they found by the tracks, he was a turpentine worker. We met him out by the Loving Pine. Before he left to go to work, he told us he was gonna come back that night and go swimming right here at the Blue Sink. So the gator man must have gotten him, too!"

"So the man by the tracks was a turpentine worker," the old man said thoughtfully. He chewed on that before he spoke again.

"And what do human gators do that regular old gators don't?" There was no sarcasm in the way he asked—no looking down on us, not even friendly teasing; just a simple question. Mr. Ambrose was the first grown-up who took seriously what Zora believed.

She beamed at him. "Well, that's the whole thing.

We're not exactly sure yet. That's why we need that book!"

"The one you saw in Lake Maitland? About gators and whatnot?"

"Everything about gators! It's called *The Myth and Lore of Gator Country*, and I know it can help us! There's a picture on the cover of a giant gator coming straight out at you, and he has a horrible expression on his face, way too smart for any regular gator. If that book's not about gators and gator men, I don't know what is."

"And this gator man, you know him?"

"That's the thing," she whispered. "It's Mr. Pendir!"

Mr. Ambrose raised his eyebrows in surprise.

"I don't know how he does it," Zora said. "But he can go from being a regular old man like you to being a walking and talking gator. I know because I was out here one night, and I saw him standing on his porch with a gator snout instead of a head. I saw him just as plain as I'm seeing you." And she pointed toward Mr. Pendir's house as she spoke.

"You think old Pendir, who lives a hop, skip, and a jump away from here, is really a gator?"

"A human gator, if only I could get my hands on that book and read about it," Zora said.

"So, Snidlets, I heard your side. Loud and clear. You ready to hear what I think about all this murder and gator business?"

Zora nodded. A breeze on the water tugged at the old man's line. He didn't bother to check it.

"The coloreds in Eatonville ain't never caused nobody no problems. But niggers killin' niggers makes white folks jumpy. And when white folks are jumpy, they can reach up awfully high — so high, a few niggers will surely end up swinging from trees. And I don't want to see no one I like dead, colored or white."

"You think more folks will end up dead?" Zora almost whispered.

My throat got tight.

"Snidlets, I ain't worried about men turning into gators. Old Pendir's been here a long time for him to suddenly start acting like a gator.

"But these turpentine workers — they're another story. They walking knots. And wherever they settle, they seem to tie everything else up in knots with 'em. I just don't want to see no one hanging from a tree. 'Cause it's good sturdy knots that lands niggers there, too."

While the old man spoke, I thought about everything I ever saw hang from a tree that didn't naturally belong there. I had seen dresses and slacks dangling off branches. I had seen hats and under-clothes swing in the wind. Many's the time I had hung my own lunch pail on a tree's bough.

Trees were everywhere in Eatonville, and I loved them as much as Zora did. The turpentine industry depended on them. Firewood was how we survived. During hurricane season, we had all experienced trees falling down or heard about a tree falling down on somebody, but it seemed a shame to me that grown men had it in them to use trees for their crimes.

As these thoughts filled my mind, Mr. Ambrose began to pack up. "Well, Snidlets, I reckon this is all the fishing and listening an old man can stand for one day. Why don't we all head home before the sun sets and makes things seem scarier than they already are?"

CHAPTER FIFTEEN

Zora's story about Mr. Pendir wasn't a lie. It was her way of making things make sense, explaining our lives through a story. And just as stories guard the pictures of the selves and worlds we cherish the most, sometimes we have to defend our stories. Monday at recess was one of those times.

Stella Brazzle led the enemy force.

The boys were kicking a ball around the yard, playing every man for himself. We girls skipped rope in the grass, singing songs that mostly Zora had made up. We always played partners, and the rule was that one pair turned while another pair jumped. When Zora and I turned for Stella and Hennie Clarke, our voices kept time perfectly. We were so good, they stayed in the rope for at least fifty jumps.

"I saw Pendir with a gator snout,
Looking his way 'bout wore me out.
But Mama's little child got good, strong eyes.
Mama's little girl don't tell no lies.
Mama's little girl don't tell no lies."

When it was our turn to skip and Stella's and Hennie's duty to turn, the song they sang punched us in the gut:

"No one saw Pendir with no gator snout,
That's a big ol' lie — there is no doubt.
Some of Mama's children got lying eyes.
Everybody knows that Zora lies.
Everybody knows that Zora lies."

We had stopped skipping rope after the first line, but we let Stella and Hennie finish their song. We wanted to hear how it ended so we would know how hard to hit them. As soon as they stopped, I went after Hennie, and Zora went after Stella. Teddy abruptly left the boys' kickball game to come over and see what was happening, and the rest of the boys followed right behind him.

"What they do to y'all?" Teddy yelled out to Zora and me. Zora didn't hear him but answered his question nonetheless.

"Who you calling a liar?" Zora yelled as she charged Stella, tackling her from behind and yanking her thick braid. Then she paused, considering whether or not she was going to push Stella's face into a mound of moist soil.

Stella blithered at the prospect of eating dirt, while the boys chanted, "Fight, fight." Hearing the commotion, Mr. Calhoun ran from inside the schoolhouse and pulled Zora off Stella.

"I don't tell lies," Zora shot at Stella, the defeated girl struggling to her feet. Zora squirmed in Mr. Calhoun's firm grasp. "I tell stories, and one of these days, all y'all are going to find out they true! My stories are true!"

When I walked Zora home, her even dirtier than usual, both of us knowing she'd have to tell her mother about getting in a fight, we assumed that her bottom had an appointment with a switch off the chinaberry tree.

That didn't happen, for a reason we could never have guessed.

* * *

There was a package waiting for Zora. It had been hand-delivered from the bookseller in Lake Maitland. Mrs. Hurston was so surprised at the arrival of a package for her youngest daughter that when Zora started to tell her story about what happened at recess, Mrs. Hurston just waved a hand for Zora to stop. She didn't have it in her to wait through the listening or give a whipping. She just handed Zora the brown-paper package and looked at her expectantly.

Zora held the bundle in her hands and stared at it. She read her name and address to herself, three times, like she needed to convince herself it was really meant for her. She gave me a *What should I do?* look, but I just shrugged. I'd never gotten a letter from anybody, let alone a package.

She handed it to her mama, who set it on the table, carefully untied the soft white twine, unfolded and opened the heavy brown paper, and lifted out of it a rich green volume.

Zora gazed at the book. She turned it to see the marvelous spine, and around to see the marbling of the page edges. Then she opened the cover.

Snidlets, the inscription read, *knowledge unties knots.*

CHAPTER SIXTEEN

At the end of school the next day, we told Teddy to meet us at the Loving Pine after he was done with his chores. We had serious business to discuss.

When he finally scootched down next to me under the awning of the Loving Pine, I realized how much I'd been missing his company. Even though I'd seen him in school that day and the day before, something about Teddy nicked my heart with longing. We were almost all alone together except for Zora. It occurred to me that, for a very long time, I had wanted just that: to be all alone with Teddy.

I didn't want to kiss him or anything lovey-dovey.

I just wanted to watch how he looked at the sky and put his hands in his pockets when he wasn't trying to impress anybody, when he was just being himself.

"What's that?" Teddy reached for the brown-paper parcel Zora had meticulously rewrapped and tied, but she held it out of reach.

"Just wait."

So we told him the whole story of how we had discovered the book in Lake Maitland, and about what Mr. Ambrose said, and how the book was waiting for Zora when we got back to her house after the fight at recess with Stella Brazzle and Hennie. Zora did most of the telling, but I put in a lot of details she forgot. Teddy listened with big-eyed attention.

Zora put up her right hand. "Before we go any further—do you both swear to keep the secrets we know, and the secrets we learn?"

We put up our right hands. "We swear."

"All right, then." Zora untied the twine holding the book, unfolded the paper with the same care she'd shown the day before, picked up the book, and held the cover for Teddy to see. His eyes bugged when he saw *The Myth and Lore of Gator Country* stamped on the front and the picture beneath it, but this time he knew better than to reach for the book.

Zora opened the book in her lap. She ran her finger down the table of contents. "Listen to this!"

Zora turned to a page somewhere in the middle of the big book. She started to read out loud.

"This is called 'The Envious Gator King.'"

"'Once upon a time,'" Zora began, "'there was a gator named Cane. He was twenty feet long and weighed nearly a ton. Besides his extraordinary length and prodigious weight'"—Zora spoke the long words slowly, savoring them on her tongue—"'there were other salient features by which Cane differed from other gators. For one, his scales were not green, like those of gators who make their home in algae-laden waters. Nor were they brown or black, like the scales of those gators who bask beneath the shade of overlying trees. Cane's scaly armor was bone-white, and he floated around his swamp like a maleficent ghost.'" Zora's voice trailed off after the last word.

"Do you think," Zora asked, "Cane could be related to Ghost?"

"But Cane is white, and we've seen Ghost with our own eyes and he wasn't white," I said. "He was plain old dark green."

"That don't mean they can't be related," Teddy said. "Look at Hennie Clarke's mother. She real light-skinned while Hennie is chocolate brown. Color difference don't mean folks ain't related. Why can't the same go for gators?"

"You're right," Zora said, her eyes thoughtful and serious. She picked up where she'd left off.

"'Whereas his fellow crocodilians blended easily into the swamp water, Cane had no cover, nor could he ever hide. But standing out against the greens and browns of the Floridian swamp was not his only vexation. Cane was plagued by envy, and in this he bore a greater resemblance to humans than he did to his own species.

"'When Cane beheld other gators, he had the same look in his onyx eyes as do human hunters. For he wanted not his brethren's friendship or their company, but their very skin. The rare times he saw a gator of his gargantuan proportions, he eviscerated his fellow reptile and attempted to drape the creature's lifeless pelt around his own. The other gators so feared Cane that, in hopes of appeasing him, they crowned him their king. But everywhere that King Cane looked, he saw not his reptilian domain but only that which he did not possess.

"'One day Cane made a decision. If he could not be brown and green like the rest of the gators, he could at least have the other thing he most coveted: song. He began his hunt by swallowing birds whole. Soon he had a whole array of songs and voices to choose from, but he found the chirps and squawks far from satisfying. He realized that what he most wanted to hear when he opened his mouth was a human voice.

"'From that day forward, Cane spent his days and nights hunting for the perfect voice. He cut off heads and tore out throats with his razor-sharp teeth to extract the voice he sought, but always in vain. For each time he tried to sing with a borrowed voice, all that came out were the moans of his wretched victims.'"

Teddy and I didn't move a muscle. Zora continued, rushing now to the end.

"'King Cane's reign of terror lasted over a hundred years. When he finally died, heavy with disappointment at not achieving his life's goal, his bone-white body sank to the bottom of the swamp. On its way down, his skin came loose from his skeleton like a giant cracked eggshell, releasing Cane's covetous spirit into the air.

"'Until this day, Cane's spirit still searches for and possesses the bodies of other gators who, like him, are different from their gator brethren. Those he would make kings are all distinguished by great size, unique coloration, or some other aberration. And they continue Cane's hunt for the perfect human voice.'"

At the end of the story, neither Teddy nor I spoke.

Zora herself then broke the silence. "I think there's a gator king right here in Eatonville."

I didn't know what to say. Zora had seen Mr. Pendir with a gator snout, and here in our hands was a book that began to explain how that was possible. "You think Mr. Pendir is one of them?" I asked. "You think he's a possessed gator king out to steal people's voices?"

Teddy tugged at a string on his shirt, mulling the situation over. "It don't say anything about gator kings being half human. It just says they're different colors and sizes."

"But it also don't say they can't be," Zora countered defensively. "It says 'other aberrations'—being half gator, half man has got to be the biggest aberration there is! And remember, he stole the head of a man with the most beautiful voice."

"Sonny didn't have a particularly fine voice," I added. "But he talked big and loud about beating gators."

"What about Old Lady Bronson?" Teddy asked.

Zora raised her eyebrows. "Could be she was in the wrong place at the wrong time, and with her crackly old voice she wasn't worth dragging down."

Teddy had no answer to that, so Zora smoothed the page of her book and resumed reading.

"'Sometimes, in the haunted hours twixt midnight and dawn, on the edge of a gator king's swamp, the souls of his many maimed and murdered victims can be heard moaning softly in unison. This, paradoxically, leads to the only reputed method of stopping a gator king's murderous rampage.'"

"What?" I asked, breathless with curiosity.

Zora pressed on. "'Go, in those hours, to a place where a gator king has been known to wreak his havoc. When you hear the moans of his victims, answer them with a lullaby. If the gator king is in earshot, your song will paralyze the beast, compel him to liberate the souls in his thrall, and send him to his watery resting place. The end.'"

"Hey," said Teddy. "If the gator king hears you singing, won't he just come and steal your voice, too?"

Zora shook her head. "Not if it's a lullaby you're singing." Her voice was tired, and her eyes wider than I had ever seen them. "It has to be a lullaby." She closed the book like she was keeping its wisdom safe between the green covers and clutched it against her chest over her heart. "You know what this means, don't you?"

"What?" Teddy and I answered in unison.

"We have to go to the Blue Sink tonight, listen for the moaning victims, and sing them a lullaby. That's the only way we can liberate Sonny's and Ivory's spirits and send the gator king to his final rest," Zora declared.

"OK," said Teddy, cottoning to the adventure. "But we need a plan."

"I'm getting to it." I wasn't sure she had been, really, but it took her only as long as my thought to come up with what sounded like one. "Carrie, you have the sweetest voice, so you gonna do the singing. Teddy, you the strongest, so bring the biggest stick you can find in case the gator king comes after us and we need to whomp him one. But be careful—if it is Mr. Pendir, he's already survived an attack by *three* gators. Even if you just stun him long enough for us all to climb up a tree, it could save our lives!"

For a second I thought about the gator king trying to steal *my* voice, but then I pictured Teddy crashing a tree branch on the gator's head and us scrambling out of the way.

"And what about you, Colonel?" Teddy asked. "You gonna wait for us back at the fort?"

"I'm gonna bring this here book," she said, patting it. "Everything we need to know is right in here." Then she got even more serious. "Wait a little while, till you know everybody in your house is good and asleep. Then sneak out real quiet, and come to Blue Sink as fast as you can. I know I don't want to be waiting out there by myself late at night, full moon or no!"

"Ain't you scared?" I asked. I meant to say "I'm scared," but it didn't come out that way.

"Yes," she answered. "But we have to do it, scared or not."

Teddy couldn't resist. "Well, actually," he said, "I'm not."

The three of us burst out laughing, and I felt the weight of sadness lift slightly in me for the first time since Ivory died. We would be the looking and finding folks like in his song. We would look for his spirit and find it, and we would set it free. I just hoped that the gator king, whoever he was, knew enough to be paralyzed by my singing, not tempted by it!

CHAPTER SEVENTEEN

That night I lay in bed and waited for the soft sound of my mama's breathing. Normally the sound lulled me to sleep, but I was too nervous to feel anything like sleepy.

I never had runaway fantasies. I never pictured myself creeping out of my bed in the middle of the night and tiptoeing out of the house so I could join the circus or the gypsies or the traveling medicine show. Knowing firsthand what my father's leaving did to my mama, I couldn't imagine anything worse you could do to a person than leaving without telling. But that's just what I did. I got up in the middle of the night and crept away, while my mama slept the deep sleep she'd earned on the pallet next to mine.

It had just finished raining. Grass slimed my ankles and calves. Crickets chirruped. Then a water moccasin slithered by fast like a streak of black lightning, making me jump. As I groped for my balance, the tree branches began to move all at once with the force of an angry parent's switch, and the fear of getting caught or, worse, of my mama waking up and finding me gone, steadied me. I knew there was a moon that night, but the sky was so cloudy I couldn't see it. For near a quarter mile I could hardly breathe. I felt confused, like the world had tilted. A place I had visited my whole life looked like no place I'd ever been. I don't know how I made it to Blue Sink.

When I finally found it, Zora and Teddy were already there, lying on their stomachs in the wet stretch of grass between Pendir's house and Blue Sink's bank. In fact, I found them by tripping over Teddy's big feet.

"Lay down here between us," Zora whispered. I did. My heart almost stopped when I looked over and saw something big lying right next to Teddy on the other side.

"What's —?"

Teddy gestured to it casually. "That's my clobbering stick. Just in case."

Zora snorted. "Small tree, more like. You should have seen him drag it over here. Now that all three of us are here," she said, "let's start."

"Start what?" I knew what we were here to do, but darkness had written Eatonville in a strange, frightening language, and I couldn't read it.

"We're going to start singing to the spirits," Teddy answered, a put-on confidence framing the edge of his words. "How about 'Washed in the Blood of the Lamb'?"

Zora shook her head. "That ain't a lullaby. A lullaby is something you sing to a baby, something sweet to make him —"

"Oh, like 'Shortenin' Bread'," said Teddy.

Zora sighed. "I suppose 'Shortenin' Bread' *is* a lullaby, but I was thinking of a song that —"

Now it was my turn to interrupt. "I have one. I have the right one."

Dark as it was, I could feel Zora's and Teddy's eyes on me.

"Well, go on, then," said Zora, taking my hand. "Start singing."

"Yeah, you start and we'll just come in," Teddy said tenderly, and he took my other hand.

I closed my eyes and imagined myself in bed, my daddy next to me with his hand on my head, smoothing my hair while he sang.

"Sleep, little pretty one, hush, now, hush,
Mama gonna hold you till the mornin'.
Sleep, little pretty one, shush, now, shush,
Mama gonna hold you till the dawnin'.

You'll never know hunger
And you'll never know fright,
Pappy work all day so you can sleep at night.
You'll never know cold
And you'll never know fear,
Pappy work all day so you can sleep now, dear.

So sleep, little pretty one, hush, now, hush,
Mama gonna hold you till the mornin'.
Sleep, little pretty one, shush, now, shush,
Mama gonna hold you till the dawnin'.

The more we sang, the more noise the swamp made. It was like we had sounded an alarm and were waking up everything in it. Fish jumped out of the water, their splashes blasting in our ears like explosions. The Spanish moss began to shake, caught up in a gust of wind, like a giant angrily tossing his hair. I thought maybe the tree would pull up its roots, stand on its sinews like legs, and pluck up all three of us in its branchy claws. But we kept singing, holding hands tight. All the while we still waited for a sign of the gator man.

Then we heard it. All of us heard it. I don't know if fear or magic was getting the best of us, but we all heard a voice—soft and eerie as the wind calling to us. We stopped singing at the exact same second, on the very same word. The moment we did, all the fear I'd been carrying lifted me up and pulled me from Teddy and Zora. I thought the voice was Ivory's, and I ran—I didn't know where, or why, but I was running too fast to breathe.

Then the ground gave away and I was flying. No, I was falling; I fell, quick and slow at the same time. I didn't know where I had landed until Zora called my name, her voice coming from somewhere above me. I had run clear over the edge of Blue Sink and landed on a hard bed of mud and rocks. The same place we'd found Old Lady Bronson.

My left shoulder hurt something terrible. The last thing I remember after that was Zora and Teddy standing right over me. "Carrie, are you all right?" Zora was saying. "Please, Carrie," she begged. "Please be all right!"

Standing right behind them was a much taller figure.

CHAPTER EIGHTEEN

W e hadn't just been imagining things. We had heard a voice. It was Mr. Pendir's.

He carried me up Blue Sink's rocky, slippery hill and all the way to the Hurstons' house. In his arms, with Zora and Teddy nearby, I was in too much pain to question anything.

When we got to the Hurston house, Zora and Teddy guided Mr. Pendir to the dining room, where he laid me on the table. By then I was singing like I had a brand-new pair of lungs and was trying them out for the very first time. In my addled state, I was still singing to set Ivory's spirit free.

"I went down to the gypsy
To get my fortune told,
She said what's lost is lost
Even if it's got a home. . . .
feel all alone . . .
feel so alone . . .
looking and finding folks
Feel all alone . . ."

Teddy held my right hand and tried to shush me, but sweetly, very sweetly. His eyes were shiny with tears. He squeezed my hand, and some water spilled out of his eyes. I stopped singing and held on to his hand.

Mrs. Hurston came rushing into the dining room with a candlestick, Sarah right behind her.

"What in the world?" Mrs. Hurston asked. "Mr. Pendir?"

Mr. Pendir was a slim, bald, pecan-brown man. His voice was gentle and a little hoarse, like a soft humming machine that didn't get much use, but it was also gentle and comforting to listen to.

"I heard these kids outside my house. Then this one here," he said, nodding his head down at me, "she ran right over the edge."

Mrs. Hurston was at my side immediately.

"Y'all better be glad Daddy ain't here," Sarah said. "If he was, he'd a ripped a tree up out the ground by now and would be whipping y'all with the roots!"

Zora ignored her sister. "Just help Carrie, Mama!" she whispered. "Just help her!"

"Where does it hurt, baby?" Mrs. Hurston asked softly.

Despite the hammering pain, I was beginning to come back to myself. "My shoulder," I said in a voice that sounded like a mouse squeak. The power it had when I was singing had gone. I felt weak. I could hardly feel anything besides Teddy holding my hand.

Mrs. Hurston turned her ear so it was right up close to my lips. "What did you say, child?"

"It's her shoulder, Mama," said Zora. "Look!"

She didn't have to ask which one. Zora told me later that my two shoulders looked like a pair of steps framing my head, the left considerably lower than my right.

"Mr. Pendir," Mrs. Hurston instructed, "we're gonna have to set this bone together. You hold her left arm against her body real tight."

Mr. Pendir took hold of my arm and pressed it into my rib cage. I didn't yell out, but I began streaming tears. I was too awake for my own good. I wished

I was asleep, but there was no use in trying. The pain was too much.

"Got her tight?" Mrs. Hurston asked Pendir.

"Yes," he answered.

Then Mrs. Hurston started grunting. I couldn't stand to watch her face contort, so I closed my eyes and started to sing again. From underneath my armpit she pulled the left side of my body up with as much force as I had ever felt. Barely five feet tall, Lucy Hurston was a testament to big strength coming in dainty packages. When my left shoulder was flush with the right one, Mrs. Hurston herself started singing.

"This girl ain't gone be lopsided," she sang. "Both her arms gone swing the same. Both her arms gone swing the same!"

Mr. Pendir wandered off into the kitchen and came back with a piece of firewood. He took it and made me a splint on the spot.

Zora spoke directly to Mr. Pendir for the first time. "How'd you know to do that?"

Mr. Pendir shrugged. "Just carpentry. Setting bones and the like ain't no different than building anything else. You always got to make sure what you're working is plumb—put straight."

* * *

We all had been put straight. Mr. Pendir wasn't a monster, much less a gator man. There he was in the Hurston home, humble and helpful. Mrs. Hurston warmed him a cup of coffee in the embers of the hearth, and he smiled in shy thanks. He was simply a man, a citizen of Eatonville.

And fully human.

CHAPTER NINETEEN

My injury hurt Zora more than it hurt me. Besides receiving all the blame for me getting hurt, she thought she deserved it. Since I was laid up at home, rags wrapped around my arm and torso to keep me stable while my bones healed, it was hard for anyone to send a chiding word in my direction—even my mama, who surely had a right to.

So Zora came to visit me every afternoon, supposedly to catch me up on schoolwork, but it always started and ended with her reminding me that it was all her fault. "Nothing was worth you getting hurt," she kept saying. "Not even catching the gator king." First I tried to argue with her, and then I just rolled my eyes every time she brought it up, but I could have rolled them from here to China for all the good it did.

A week after our failed try at defeating the gator king and rescuing the souls of his victims, I was sitting on the front step, sweating through my makeshift bandages and wishing I could skip off and search out something to do. Mama couldn't miss work on the day shift, but she had asked to miss three nights so she could come home, make me dinner, and stay with me. Now that I was healing well, she had gone back to the second shift. To make up for the money she'd lost those three nights home with me, on her off nights she went and picked oranges in the grove two blocks north of the hotel, for as long as it held light. My end of the bargain was a promise to stay still and eat the corn bread and pork rind she left for my suppers.

From where I stood, the consequences of breaking my rest were too steep, anyway. I had no intention of becoming lopsided, and though I was at the point where doing nothing seemed like the hardest work I could do, I kept at it. If I didn't, I might never be any good to my mama.

Zora was later than usual, and I was going back and forth between worried and plain old lonely. Then I looked up to see . . . Teddy! Zora had said he was grounded till heaven knew when, so I hadn't expected to see him for a long time.

"Hey." He was holding out something wrapped in a towel. "My mama made it. She knows you like it."

I knew what it was without opening the towel: peanut brittle. Every year Teddy's mama made a big batch of it at Christmas, and I always got a nice-size piece. Maybe it was because I always wrote her a note to say thank you and tell her how she made the best peanut brittle I'd ever tasted. Maybe she might have sent it anyway, because she was like that. In any case this piece was twice the size of what she usually sent at Christmas. I smiled, and it felt funny. I realized that I hadn't smiled in a week.

"You gonna sit down and help me with this?" I asked. "I can't eat it all myself."

"Yeah." He smiled shyly. He dug his hand into the pocket of his overalls and pulled out something I couldn't see. "And this is from me," he said. "Put out your hand."

Into my hand he placed something the size of my palm. It was a turtle shell, empty, dry, and beautiful—

ebony black with bright yellow dots on it. It was his spotted turtle shell, the star of his windowsill.

"Teddy . . ." I kept staring at it. "You can't . . ."

He sat down, right next to me on the step. "I *want* you to have it." He took the peanut brittle, held the towel tight around it, and whapped it hard on the ground so that it cracked into pieces we could eat. He took out a piece and gave it to me. Then he took out another piece and held it up. "I will help you with this, though."

We chomped for a few minutes, not talking except to say how good it was. When Teddy stopped chewing, he stretched his legs out and asked, "How's your arm?"

"Itches."

"Don't hurt?"

"Not too much if I don't move it real quick. Or roll over on it at night."

Teddy nodded. He was looking around everywhere, except at me. "My daddy said we should never have been out there. And I keep thinking that since we was, I should have protected you."

"What *could* you have done? I bolted." I suddenly felt embarrassed. "I thought I heard a voice."

"Yeah, me too. We all did. It was Mr. Pendir. You know that, right?"

"No. I mean I do now, but I heard . . . The voice I thought I heard . . . I thought it was Ivory."

Teddy looked at me and solemnly said, "Maybe it was. Maybe we freed Ivory's soul after all."

I met his gaze. "Do you think so, Teddy? Really?"

"We did everything the book said, and there was . . . *something* strange blowing through the swamp that night. We all felt it!"

"Only I can't imagine Mr. Pendir being the gator king anymore," I confessed.

Teddy shook his head. "No," he agreed. "I've been thinking on it a lot, and I don't reckon he could be. He saved your life. Way I figure it, gator kings are in the business of taking lives, not saving them."

Some things still worried me. "But Zora said she saw Mr. Pendir with a gator snout. And he did escape from that gator attack without a scratch, way back when. If he isn't the gator king, who is?"

"I don't know. I don't know." Teddy chewed his lip. "I keep thinking maybe there isn't even a gator king at all. But then I keep thinking . . ."

"What?"

"If there isn't a gator king, then what killed Ivory?"

CHAPTER TWENTY

I'd hoped we could keep thinking on these questions with Zora, but she was late and Teddy had to get back to do his chores. When Zora finally showed up a half hour later, I hadn't gotten any further in my figuring on Ivory, and the peanut brittle was gone.

Zora walked up to the front step like she had lead in both shoes. She sat down beside me. "Why you so late?" I asked. "Where you been? You missed Teddy!"

Then she spoke quietly and completely unlike herself. "I was at the Loving Pine."

"By yourself? Why? What happened?"

"I thought I was there by myself."

I got a chill right then. "What you mean, Zora? You were either there by yourself or you weren't."

"I was at the Loving Pine, Carrie, feeling down, real down, wishing it was me got hurt instead of you. I was thinking about how maybe I was wrong about Mr. Pendir being the gator king. Then I heard something. . . ."

"What?" I was about ready to jump out of my skin, sure she was going to say she had heard Ivory's soul singin', just like I thought I had.

I had never spoken the word *believer* in my life, but that's what I was: a believer . . . in ghosts.

"You hear Ivory?"

"No, Carrie," Zora said slowly. "I didn't hear Ivory, but I heard all about him. Joe Clarke was in the woods by the Loving Pine."

"Joe Clarke? Talked to you about Ivory?"

Zora shook her head. "No, not me. Remember that lady we saw in Lake Maitland? Gold?"

"Of course," I answered. "How's she know Mr. Clarke?"

"I don't know, but she does. And what's more, Joe Clarke knew Ivory, too. And what's more . . ." She took a deep breath. "Ivory was Gold's brother."

"Say what, now?" I nearly shouted. "Ivory was colored like us! And Gold—she's white. Ain't she?"

"I don't know what she is," Zora said. "But she's not the same as other white folks."

"I don't get it. White folks think she's one of them, don't they?"

"Yeah. But from what Mr. Clarke said to her, Gold don't know who she is and don't nobody else know, either. Anyway, she said she couldn't find Ivory anywhere, and Mr. Clarke said, 'There's a reason you can't find your brother. It's because he's dead.' She freezes: 'No! No! No! He can't be dead! He can't be!' and Mr. Clarke, standing with his hands on his hips and looking real angry, says, 'Well, he can be, because he is, and I seen the body. Somebody made real sure he was dead, because they went and killed him—took his head clean off to make sure.'"

My rickety front step became a stage. Zora deepened her voice when she spoke Joe Clarke's words. She whimpered when she transformed into Gold, and clear as day I saw the beautiful woman in my mind's eye.

"Now Gold falls all to pieces—'Oh God, oh God, oh God, oh God!'" Zora was walking in a circle, wringing her hands and looking up to heaven. Then she spun around to face Joe Clarke: "'I have to take him home! I have to take him home!'

"But Joe Clarke ain't havin' none of it. 'Home? What home? You can't take that boy home 'cause you ain't got no home to take him to—mixed up with white folks as you is! To have a home to go to, a real one, you got to be unafraid to be who you are. And who you gonna take him to? That man I seen you with? I'm pretty sure you haven't told *him* who you really are!'

"And Gold gets this crazy look and starts saying, 'No, I—no, I—no, I . . .'

"And Mr. Clarke, he don't budge. He says, 'Your only pain comes from playing pretend with white folks.'" Then Zora-as-Joe got a real hard look, almost like hate but not, like equal parts pity and cold fury. "'Pity of it is, all that damage of pretending done run off you like rainwater only to soak poor Ivory to the bone.'

"Then she starts into wailing—'What do I do now? What do I do without Ivory?'" Zora-as-Gold's eyes were wild, like she was seeing a ghost and couldn't look away. Then Zora-as-Joe shook his head.

"'You were already living without him, so you'll

just go on doing that.'" Zora-as-Gold slumped down against the copper beech in front of our porch. "'Ivory . . . Ivory . . .'

"Then she set to crying hard. And Joe Clarke just stared at her for I don't know how long. Didn't say a word. And Gold looks up at him like she's pleading for her life. 'I can't,' she says, wailing. 'Please let me stay here in Eatonville with you.'

"'We Eatonville folks ain't got the fear of whites in us, and I won't allow anyone to bring that fear here. Eatonville is our home.'

"Finally he says, 'Go back to Maitland.' That's all. But he says it in this voice like the voice of Judgment Day.

"'Maybe you're wrong. Maybe Ivory's not dead,' she says. 'I have to stay here where he can find me!'

"Joe shakes his head. 'There ain't no one looking to find you now. No one worth a plugged nickel.' Then he turned and walked back in the direction of town. I expected her to get herself up and go back to Lake Maitland, but she just sat there, staring and wailing. I think she's still there crying right now. . . ."

Zora got up from the tree and sat back down next to me, breathless from her performance. I couldn't believe my ears. Gold must have been the one Ivory was looking to find. The somebody who didn't know she was lost.

Then Zora said something that spun me like a top.

"Every time I try to explain to myself what probably happened, what really happened outgrows my explanation."

I had never before seen Zora unable to fold new information into her own telling of a thing. Her doubts, coming right on top of Teddy's doubts about the gator king, shook me.

I found myself pacing in a little line, back and forth, holding my sling-bound arm against my side.

Mr. Pendir, who'd fixed my broken arm, wasn't a gator, let alone a gator king; he never was. It was impossible now to imagine that shy, gentle man killing Ivory. And if Mr. Pendir wasn't the gator king — maybe there wasn't ever even a gator king at all, like Teddy said. But that thought didn't relieve me. Instead, it filled me with a strange kind of fury. The things that before were painful were suddenly unbearable.

Zora had made me a story out of events that were too huge and too frightening for me to hold. She had put them neatly into places that let me step back and see them, name them, understand them, and do something about them.

Now she was taking that away from me, not because she was selfish or mean, but because she had a relentless curiosity. Zora's only real crime was wanting to know what we shouldn't have known, and then not knowing until it was too late that we shouldn't have known it.

I was shattered. My faith in the magic that holds the world on its axis had broken.

I wanted to cry, but I had no tears. I wanted to shout and scream instead, to tear things apart on the outside so that they looked like how I felt on the inside.

I spun on my heels and pointed my stick at Zora. "You know what? It's your fault! It's your fault, all of it! First you made up the gator king—no, first you took Ghost and made *him* into the gator king. Then every time you talked about it, the evil got kicked up higher in the air, and bad things started to happen—to Ivory and Old Lady Bronson and me! It was you who made it happen! Your words brought evil to life! It didn't have no power before you conjured it!"

I meant every word of it—even if it didn't make sense, even if I didn't believe it, any of it, an hour later.

Only years later did I understand why the death of Ivory, a man I barely knew, had rocked me like an earthquake. It seems obvious now. Any grown person with a heart would have seen it long before.

That was the day that in my gut, I finally realized that my father was gone for good. He wasn't coming back, and we weren't going to save him, any more than we could have saved Ivory.

That was the day I finally began mourning him, the day I finally allowed myself to believe that he was dead, along with all the songs and smiles and warm words that should have supported me as I grew, that should have fought off hurts that wounded me, that should have held me and cradled me and crooned in my ear, *Sleep, little pretty one, hush now, hush* . . . My daddy's love could have made Ivory's death less terrifying. It would still have been sad, even horrible, but it wouldn't have pitched all sense out of my ten-year-old world.

But that wisdom only showed itself to me in hindsight. That afternoon, as I paced back and forth in my short line, faster and faster, kicking up the dry dirt in little brown clouds around my ankles, rage shot through me. Rage. And it was all aimed at Zora.

But she didn't respond in kind. Instead of being angry back at me, instead of telling me how and why I was wrong, she looked up at me from the front step, nodded slowly, and stood. Maybe she understood what was really in my thoughts, or maybe she was having thoughts of her own. Either way, she took my hand and said, "Let's go see Gold."

CHAPTER TWENTY-ONE

At the crossroads that led either to Lake Maitland or to the woods that held the Loving Pine, Zora practically ran ahead of me. Maybe she took off because she wanted the whole business to be over with as fast as possible. I know I did, but the feeling didn't put a fire under me. It pulled at my bones with dread.

Approaching the Loving Pine we could smell and then see a little fire in the clearing just in front of the tree, but no sign of Gold. The canopy was so thick that the light of the fire made the deep shade surrounding it look like artificial night. Zora looked around and then started whistling the tune Ivory had sang to us.

There was a rustling in the trees, and Gold flew out. It was unmistakably Gold, and yet I could hardly recognize her in the flickering firelight.

Her tear-streaked face struck me most. The eyes that had seemed dark amber and round on Maitland Avenue were now hazel and catlike. Her hair wasn't just unkempt—it was ropy and heavy. She was wearing clothes I could only imagine on a rich woman—a dress made of thick brocade that rustled when she moved, and boots that looked softer than kid leather and must have been creamy white once—but they were ruined by rents and gashes and the clayey marks of the forest floor. The bridge of Gold's nose was like that of Rose Cousin, a girl in the year behind us whose whole family was so Indian, there was no point pretending. Her skin took on the warm tones of the fire, and I could see that what I had thought was a glow from within this woman was really a golden undercoat. Gold may have looked white the first time we saw her, but here by the fire, afraid, she was more colored than white—and yet not colored like us.

I recognized bits and pieces of us on her face and in her bearing, but even in the copper of the firelight, tan and all, she looked like she had been wiped down with chalk dust.

"Ivory!" she called out, staring desperately in our direction. When we stepped into the clearing, her face fell, and she crumpled to the ground like a dropped marionette.

"I thought you were someone else." She spoke to the fire, not to us.

Zora swallowed hard, then said, "You thought it was your brother."

Gold leaped up like she'd sat on a porcupine, startling us both. I put my hand to my heart.

"You know Ivory? Do you know where he is? Have you seen him?"

Zora glanced at me and then cleared her throat. "We came to talk to you because Ivory was our friend."

She looked at us incredulously. "Ivory . . . your friend?"

We nodded. "Do you mind if we set down?" Zora asked. Gold, we knew, wasn't going to be hospitable like regular folks because she wasn't in a regular folks frame of mind.

Gold didn't say anything, but gestured to the pine needles. It was like someone telling you to make yourself comfortable in your own parlor. I couldn't help but notice the fire dying, and just when I thought I couldn't fight the impulse to stir some life back into it, she picked up a stick and poked it, turning the one big piece dry-side-down. I don't know who I thought would have made the fire for her, but up until that moment it hadn't occurred to me that she herself would know how.

Gold listened calmly as Zora told her about overhearing her conversation with Joe Clarke and about our meeting Ivory before that.

Gold smiled a little, and a flash of the copper in her skin blew away a speck or two of the chalk dust. "I gave him that guitar when I was eighteen. Somebody gave it to me, and I gave it to him." Her voice no longer had the measured and ladylike confidence it had in Lake Maitland. Rather, it sounded like an echo of her carefree self. Instead of following Gold down the path of nostalgia, Zora pressed on. "Miss Gold, why did Ivory come to Eatonville looking for you?"

I didn't expect the question any more than Gold did. She took a deep breath. Her eyes were looking across the fire at us, but in her mind she was looking right into her past.

"The first thing I remember is moving day. I was

three years old, and we moved into a boardinghouse on a colored street, across from Joe Clarke's family. The Clarkes owned the boardinghouse. Joe's daddy was a stonemason, and a good one, and I guess he knew what to do with the money he made.

"That's maybe when my mama started to get sick. I'm not sure. I know that the only thing that did her any good when she got in the grip of one of her spells was Ivory's singing.

"I was fairer than my mama, and much fairer than Ivory. Sometimes she would take me downtown and pretend to be my mammy so we could buy things in stores where colored folks weren't welcome. My mama said fooling white folks was never a sin if it brought us what we needed. Ivory never liked it, but I thought it was the top! I loved bringing my mama gifts, and that's what it felt like when we got to shop where we wanted. It was like I was a skeleton key unlocking another world just for my mama."

My heart felt heavy trying to imagine folks not knowing my mama was my mama. I couldn't think of a single thing in the world I could want more than my pride in being my mama's daughter, and I felt a flush of shame for Gold.

"After my mama passed, we stayed on at the

Clarkes' boardinghouse, and Ivory got work picking and hauling and doing all kinds of things. While he was working, I would go over to Silver Springs. Some white kids took a liking to me and invited me with them to things. When Ivory found out, he was angry. I wanted to explore the world—the whole world, not just the colored world—but he would have none of it. I did it anyway. One day one of the white kids saw Ivory talking to me and thought he was an uppity nigger. So he got some boys together and beat Ivory almost senseless. Ivory got away and hid in the woods. I didn't know what to do. I ran back home and found Joe Clarke. He came with me and helped tend to Ivory's wounds." In my mind's eye, I saw a young Ivory broken and battered and curled up like a baby on the forest floor. I was glad the Ivory of the past had Joe Clarke there to help him. "After that Joe helped us out whenever he could, and sort of watched over us."

Zora put Gold's problem bluntly into words. "Why would you want to be like white folks?"

Gold looked down and spread her hands out in front of her.

"I get tired of being colored. I get tired of seeing

everything the world has to offer and settling for a bowl of nothing. With Will, nothing is off limits. . . ."

I glanced over at Zora. She sat, rapt, listening to Gold.

I couldn't stop the words from leaving my mouth. "Was Ivory nothing?"

Gold's eyes welled up with tears.

"You're both lucky. You don't have to make hard choices. You know exactly where you belong. Ivory promised my mother that he would always watch out for me, and even when I ran away from him, he was always right on my heels."

Zora spoke up then, but I could see her almost wincing at what she had to say. "Miss Gold, it seems like sticking by your people, by the people you love, is the easiest choice of all."

I imagined that Gold would rear up at that— either tell us to mind our own business or start bawling or both. But it was the opposite: Zora's words seemed to disconnect Gold from us. She stared into the fire and started talking to herself low and fast, oblivious. The chalk came to her face in an even thicker layer than it had been when we first arrived.

"I saw Ivory just over a week ago—it was a Friday.

No, it was Thursday, out by the rail switch coming into Lake Maitland. Will's been acting funny ever since that day. He must have followed me . . . just like those kids in Silver Springs did! What if Will thought Ivory was an uppity nigger? Or—or worse!" We sat completely still, letting the full meaning of her words sink in.

"He's been nervous and angry all week—asking me where I'm going, what I'm doing all day, and talking about going away for a few weeks. . . . Oh, Lord, he's so rageful, so jealous."

She stood up, wild-eyed. "Oh, God, what if Will did this? I can't go back to him! I can't!" She stood perfectly still for a moment, then the realization of what she was saying knocked her to her knees. Her hair came forward and looked, in the firelight, like it had a life of its own, like tightening twine.

"Miss Gold," Zora whispered, "where are you going to go?"

Gold got on her feet again.

"You girls need to get on home," she said, "and I have to get on, too."

We watched Gold step over the fallen bark and through the wood brush in the direction of Maitland. Both Zora and I had heard the phrase "Lay down with the devil" before, but I don't think, staring at Gold's back as she headed away from us and toward something truly dark, that we understood what it meant until that moment.

Zora grabbed my good arm and pulled me up to my feet. "Let's go home," she said.

CHAPTER TWENTY-TWO

We walked slowly, but not because of fatigue. The knowledge that Gold herself—her perspective on the world, her actions and her inactions—might have played a part in Ivory's death dropped weights on our tongues and hearts.

When we got to the road, I spoke.

"So a man stole Ivory's voice."

"Yes," Zora said with a slow nod. She had already pressed and kneaded this thought herself. "Probably a white man." She looked at me. "Probably Gold's man."

I couldn't shake the feeling, though, that Gold was just as dangerous as her white man. Her whole life, whether she knew it or not, Gold had been courting death. A white man may have killed and buried Gold's brother, Gold's keeper, but letting white folks believe the lie of her looks had made it possible.

We were sitting on a tinderbox of secrets, and didn't know how to tell someone without lighting the match ourselves.

I stumbled and sat down on the front step of Zora's house. Zora sat next to me and leaned her head against mine. I had never felt so small.

We were up against a force more powerful than white folks and more lethal than a gator king. The color of a person's skin alone could make one woman worth protecting, while it made another man fit to die.

CHAPTER TWENTY-THREE

Old Lady Bronson thought her fainting spell by the Blue Sink was an omen, but she was certain the chickens weren't coming home to roost on her doorstep. Instead she felt in her gut that somehow, for no reason at all, Mr. Pendir's house had found its way onto Death's itinerary. And that as a matter of chance, Death had merely stumbled over her on its way. So every morning since the day Zora declared Mr. Pendir half gator, Old Lady Bronson sent Miss Billie to Mr. Pendir's house to check on him.

Midmorning of the day after we found Gold in the woods, Billie Bronson went and rapped on Mr.

Pendir's door as usual. There was no answer. After a few moments, she tried the knob; it was open. Mr. Pendir's home was a four-room square house, bigger than ours, which made it still pretty small, but darker and dustier than most.

The previous few mornings, Billie had found him sitting in the threadbare chair underneath a sepia portrait of his parents — the only photograph in the house — deep asleep. That's where she expected to find him again. When she didn't see him there, she called his name softly, walking slowly through the house. The kitchen and the dining room were empty. There was only one room left: his bedroom. She opened the door and found something there she couldn't have imagined. It wasn't just Mr. Pendir lying dead in his bed, which he was — Billie didn't have any trouble imagining that. The sight was among the strangest that anyone had ever heard of in Eatonville. It was Mr. Pendir lying dead in his bed, flat on his back, fully dressed, wearing a green and sparkling gold wooden gator-snout mask. Not only that but the walls of his bedroom were covered with bobcat heads and armadillo heads and parrot faces.

All the time Mr. Pendir had lived in Eatonville knocking around his old house, alone and weary-looking, he had been making things, and the things he made were beautiful.

That's not to say that Billie Bronson understood that all right off. Billie said later that walking into Mr. Pendir's bedroom was like entering an exotic zoo full of wild animals.

Word of Mr. Pendir's passing spread through Eatonville fast. My mama used her whole half-hour of lunch just to come home around midday and tell me, so I wouldn't hear it from a stranger.

The death of Mr. Pendir, after everything we had found out about Joe Clarke, Ivory, and Gold, felt like more than I could handle; I felt like a balloon somebody had let all the air out of, then stepped on for good measure. I think it was more than Zora could handle, too.

When she got to my house for our after-school visit, she barely waved and just plopped down next to me on the front step. I was making circles in the dirt with a stick; it made me think of Gold poking the fire. We sat in silence; there was only one thing on both our minds.

"You hear about him?" she asked after a few minutes. She stared at her knee, picking at a scab.

I nodded.

"Everything?" she asked.

"I guess."

She leaned in for a closer look at her knee. "Poor Mr. Pendir."

I traced another circle in the dirt.

"I suppose now folks know I wasn't lying about Mr. Pendir's gator head."

I looked at her for the first time since she sat down. "Me and Teddy always believed you."

She closed her eyes and put her head on her knee.

After a few minutes she opened them and sat up.

"Come on," I said. "Let's go for a walk."

CHAPTER TWENTY-FOUR

W e walked in silence, the weight of our knowledge hanging on our shoulders like wet wool blankets. We still didn't have a glimmer of an idea of what to do with what we knew about Gold and Ivory and poor Mr. Pendir. Without paying much attention at all, we made our way to a nearby lagoon. We sat on the edge of the lagoon braiding moss. A cheerful whistling hit our backs. It was old Mr. Ambrose come to fish.

"Afternoon, Mr. Ambrose," we said.

"Afternoon, ladies."

"Oh, Mr. Ambrose, did you get my letter?" Zora asked.

"Yes, I did, Snidlets."

"Thank you so much for that beautiful book," she said. "I never got such a nice gift!"

"Well, it was my pleasure. Was it everything you'd hoped it would be?"

"Oh, yes, it—" Zora shot me an apologetic look, like she was saying sorry for pretending that things were fine. But she didn't have to. I understood—white lies. "It had everything you could ever want to know about gators and . . ."

"And gator kings?"

"Yes, and everything about gator kings, too."

Mr. Ambrose looked at her. "Mm-hm. Why's your face so long?"

"Oh, no reason." Zora's voice was so hollow it couldn't have convinced a stranger, let alone someone who'd known her since before she knew herself. He recognized her ailment exactly.

"There are two kinds of hearts," he said after a time. "There's the ones that don't got nothing in them. And there's others that need to pour their feelings out. Now, since I know you got a mighty strong light beating in your chest, why don't you tell me what's weighing on you?"

By this time the old man was sitting beside Zora.

His sunburned face was etched with craggy, honest lines. Zora's eyes got glassy. The agony of having to decide what to do cut her. I knew Zora almost better than I knew myself, but I wasn't sure whether she was going to tell the old man what she heard between Gold and Joe Clarke or not. Mr. Ambrose was definitely an ally, but he was also white.

"How do you know you can trust someone?" Zora asked. Of course the old man knew that Zora was asking whether or not she could trust him. He met her eyes.

"When you help bring a person into this world, Snidlets, you have a bond. Most folks meet after they've been around for a while, and maybe seen a little too much. But when we met, Snidlets, you were brand, spanking new. Whenever I look at your face, I can't help but see you as a baby. With a person who can see your baby self, you don't have anything to be afraid of.

"The folks you have in your mind as bundles in their mothers' arms, you always want to keep safe. Always."

Zora trusted this old white man, and I was pretty sure I did, too.

"It's just that I don't want anyone to get hung from a tree," Zora blurted out. I don't think she had even considered such a thing possible until she said it. But that was the largest portion of Zora's burden, her knowledge and the power that gave her—the power to have a hand in hurting someone.

"Snidlets, I don't want that to happen, neither," Mr. Ambrose said, wearing a look more troubled than it was curious. That distinction mattered.

Zora told Mr. Ambrose everything she heard at the Loving Pine, and she finally began to cry. The old man became stiff. He wanted to comfort her, but didn't quite know how. He looked like he was going to hug her, but then had a better idea.

Mr. Ambrose reached into his front pocket and pulled out a clean white handkerchief. He offered it to Zora gently, but she was so soaked with sorrow that the gesture was lost on her. We all stared gloomily at the pine needles and leaves floating atop the lagoon.

I don't know how to explain that moment except to say that, before the moving pictures and before the radio, folks were accustomed to silence; we even used to hug up on it once in a while. I never thought of it as special then, that we could just sit and stare and luxuriate in the comfort of our own thoughts. Without time to think, we wouldn't have had anything to talk about in the first place.

But the time it took for Mr. Ambrose to speak up again felt long, even for then.

"Only very special people can put real-life puzzles with human pieces together," he finally said. "You're one of those folks, Snidlets. You got a brain in your head there ain't no match for—way smarter than algebra. You also got the feelings in your gut to go with it. It's a gift for you to share. Don't be stingy with what you know, but be sure of the folks you're sharing it with. You did the right thing by telling me and not too many other folks."

"I think so," Zora agreed. "But I'm scared."

"Only a fool," he answered, "wouldn't be terrified by the weight of what you know and what you feel. From the day I met you, I thought you could become a lot of things. A fool wasn't one of them."

The air vibrated around us. It felt like a christening or baptism, but choirs and a preacher and pews weren't necessary. Mr. Ambrose had just showed Zora to her seat of power, and it wasn't in a back row.

"I'm sending you on a very important mission," Mr. Ambrose said. "Go to Joe Clarke and tell him everything you heard. Don't hold anything back. Also, tell him that you told me, and that I respect him very much. Say I know that he will make sure justice is done in Eatonville. The same as I will make sure justice is done in Lake Maitland."

The old man gathered the fishing gear he never set up and headed home. Zora and I walked away from the lagoon lighter in step than we had arrived. Having great responsibility was one thing. Knowing what to do with it was another. And though we hadn't gone far from home, neither of us returned the same girls we had been when we left.

CHAPTER TWENTY-FIVE

The following afternoon, we went to Joe Clarke's store.

We knew we had a mission, and we knew we couldn't breathe a word about it.

I thought about Gold. No matter how bad she felt now, she couldn't change what had happened.

When we got to Joe Clarke's store, the usual cast of characters stood on the porch interrupting one another. Mr. Clarke was leaning against a post as usual, but he didn't look right as rain. He leaned like a powerful tree taking a long overdue rest. The look in his eyes was far from peaceful.

Zora spoke. "Can I talk to you, Mr. Clarke?"

The chorus went silent.

"'Course you can," he said. He seemed to welcome the distraction.

"Don't do it, Joe," someone called out. "They only want to take you for more licorice!"

"No, we don't." Zora said it so calmly that Mr. Clarke could tell she was dead serious.

He ushered us into the store and led us to the small office in the back. The desktop was covered in papers—receipts, bills of lading, and long sheets of numbers in rows. I looked at the shiny varnished legs of the desk. They held the shape of sturdy branches.

Zora dove into the conversation like skipping rope; she just jumped right in. "I overheard you talking with Gold out by the Loving Pine."

Mr. Clarke stared at Zora for a moment, taken aback. "What did you say, child?"

"I heard you and Gold talking in the woods on Tuesday. We went to see her that evening to tell her Ivory had been looking for her. We wanted to help lay his spirit to rest." Zora looked at Mr. Clarke. He was still just staring at her.

She pressed on. "Then Gold starts wailing and tells us how jealous her white man is, that white man she goes with in Lake Maitland." Zora paused. "She thinks he maybe killed Ivory."

Joe Clarke was at a loss for words. Zora, sensing his shock, talked more and faster.

"We haven't told a soul, Mr. Clarke. Not until yesterday when we saw old Mr. Ambrose by the lagoon. I told him everything 'cause he helped bring me into this world, and you can trust someone who done a big thing like that for you. And he said you could trust him, too. He told me to tell you that he knew you would do justice in Eatonville. He wanted you to know that he'll do justice in Lake Maitland."

Joe Clarke sat back in his chair, looking winded. None of us spoke. Then he stood up and turned his back to us for a long minute. When he turned around again, he looked like his old self.

I was so relieved that I burst into a grin, but Zora wasn't so quick to end our talk. She wanted more answers. Now that we knew who Gold and Ivory were, and how Joe Clarke knew them, and maybe who had taken Ivory's life, there was one piece of the puzzle still missing. And Zora, determined to know everything, demanded the final answer.

"What about Mr. Pendir? Did he want to be a gator more than a man?"

Mr. Clarke looked at us thoughtfully before answering.

"Yes and no," Joe Clarke said, squinting. "Pendir got dealt more hurt than he knew how to play. He lost his mama and daddy early on. His mama's family were poor sharecroppers and they didn't need another mouth to feed, so he was raised working for white folks, but like a slave, not like a child. He grew up feeling like a whipping post. He was grown when he heard about Eatonville and came here, hoping there was enough work from colored folks that he'd never have to deal with white folks again. At first folks tried to bring him into the circle of town life, but he just couldn't put his hurt and mistrust away. He knew how to work wood, but he never learned how to be friendly with folks, and never learned how to let folks be friendly with him. He kept to himself and after a while folks got used to hiring him for work, but otherwise leaving him be."

Mr. Clarke stood and stretched his big bones. "This desk right here, Mr. Pendir made it for me. He was blessed with the power to take plain wood—scraps too small to be worth much to anyone—and carve them and shape them and paint them into something else."

He reached into a drawer and drew out a lion mask so detailed that Zora and I gasped. "Mr. Pendir breathed life into wood. When his fears threatened to swallow him up, he faced them down with the masks he made. His art scared off his fear."

I thought about Mr. Pendir missing his mama and daddy, and I wondered if I had anything beautiful to make inside myself that would still my own fears. Then I thought about Gold. She and Mr. Pendir had something in common. They both felt afraid and cheated by the cards life had dealt them, but they took that fear and channeled it in different ways. Mr. Pendir took his fear inside and locked himself into a room alone. Gold hid her fear inside and walked away from where she came from and everything she knew. Both of them ended up alone.

The bad things that happen to you in life don't define misery — what you do with them does. When Mr. Pendir and Gold could have chosen connection, they chose solitude; when they could have brought loving themselves to loving someone else, they wore masks instead and shunned love's power. You can't hide from life's pain, and folks that love you would never expect you to.

Zora and I sat with that a moment. Joe Clarke's

lips spread across his face in a closed-mouth smile. It was a sad smile, but reassuring.

"I'm going to do justice, girls, but sometimes justice works better in silence. You didn't do wrong to tell me and Mr. Ambrose. But don't tell anyone else what you know. Let justice take its course now."

When we reappeared on the front porch of Joe's store, our pockets and mouths full of licorice sticks, the men of Eatonville broke into an uproar.

"Joe, you let these two little girls sucker you into giving them treats again," one man said.

"Watch out, Joe," said another. "These two gonna leave you bankrupt!"

"Giving don't got a thing to do with going bankrupt," Joe Clarke answered. "Holding back does."

CHAPTER TWENTY-SIX

B ack at the Hurstons' house, we sat silently on the shady porch, the licorice divided neatly between us, steadily chewing our treats.

We didn't savor the licorice sticks the same way we did when we were rewarded for finding Old Lady Bronson. Of course the candy was sweet, and it was still delicious, but it didn't seem like one of life's treasures anymore, let alone the sweetest.

I knew much more than I wanted to about so-called shortcuts in life, and senseless violence, and chasing down someone you love. I knew that death was death. I knew that outside the boundaries of Eatonville, it could be dangerous not to be white, and that inside those boundaries was no guarantee of safety.

A wind rustled its way through the chinaberry tree. After about twenty minutes Mrs. Hurston, carrying baby Everett and a basket full of oranges, came up the walk. With her came the scent of citrus and gardenias.

"Carrie, your mama just gave me these oranges," she said. When she got closer to the porch, she stopped, turned her head, and cut her eyes. "What on earth possessed Joe Clarke," she asked, "to laden you two down with all this candy?"

The timing couldn't have been more perfect. It was rare to have quiet around the Hurston house, and Zora took full advantage. Joe Clarke had asked us not to tell. We knew how to keep a secret, but Zora's mother was always the one exception. Right there on the front porch, with us still sitting and Mrs. Hurston standing with baby Everett asleep on her left shoulder, Zora and I together told her everything.

Every expression under the sun passed across Mrs. Hurston's face. I was certain she was going to drop the basket of oranges. She didn't, and she also kept silent until we were finished. Her first response was to place the basket on the ground. Then she sat down

right between us. Neither of us thought twice about
the flattened licorice.

Mrs. Hurston, close to tears, placed Everett
upright in her lap and put an arm around each of us.
I felt the smidgen of tight feeling still left in my chest
disappear.

Until that moment, I believed that what I carried
inside of me was just myself and nothing of other
people, not even the ones I loved. If I ever had the
nerve to open up my heart, I thought I'd be faced with
nothing but a tall, round-faced brown girl with coal-
black hair. I felt that alone.

But on the hem of this experience, wrapped in
Mrs. Hurston's embrace, I got up the nerve to take a
peek into my heart, and to my surprise I didn't find
that lonely picture of myself. What I found there was
much bigger. I found all of Eatonville.

There was a picture of Blue Sink on the clearest
sunny day. There was a picture of Joe Clarke's porch
and all the shenanigans that went on there. The Loving Pine stood tall and affectionate as ever. There was
the memory of my own parents, sitting holding hands
on our front step. And I saw myself with Teddy, doing
exactly the same thing someday. Of course Zora and

Mrs. Hurston were in my heart too, snuggled under a light-as-air white blanket in Mrs. Hurston's feather bed.

After taking a good long look inside myself, I also knew that my heart didn't belong to me. I wasn't even its landlord. The people, dirt, trees, bricks, and air of Eatonville were. Eatonville wasn't just my home. It was my destiny.

EPILOGUE

The justice that old Mr. Ambrose and Joe
Clarke said they would see to was achieved,
in retrospect, swifter than an arrow.

Mrs. Jefferson, who had hinted at Gold's real iden-
tity in the first place, began whispering to folks that
the bride-to-be was indeed passing. For three weeks,
Negroes watched Gold doggedly.

A woman said that Gold gave her the evil eye
one day, and the next day she broke her foot. A man
referred to Gold's cords of blond hair as a lynch rope.
A week or so later, someone cut the yellow-haired tail
off that man's only horse and threw it in his front yard.
Every day there was a new episode. No one thought

her mixed blood was the problem; the problem was that she saw her own people as a liability.

So when Joe Clarke took a trip home to Orlando to visit with family for a few days, no one seemed to notice that Gold's departure coincided with Joe's trip. Folks were just glad to have the bad omen gone. But I knew that Mr. Clarke was behind the end of the scandal. For that matter, I knew Zora and I were, too.

As for William—Gold's man, Ivory's likely murderer—his business dried up inside of a few months. He left his new home in Lake Maitland, ruined and broken, before the end of autumn.

So two men, one black and one white, both protecting the sanctity of our peaceful world, had dispensed justice in a way so quiet that only five people in total ever knew about it. Joe Clarke and Mr. Ambrose had done in grown folks' terms what Zora and I had done with our childhood fantasy—rooted out evil and laid crooked tracks straight.

Eatonville was never the same for me after that. My child self belonged to the world of the gator king, to the Eatonville of our childhood fantasies. Whether that world was real or not doesn't matter. It was true. And though it no longer exists outside of me or Zora's stories, I still visit the memories.

Zora loved Eatonville every bit as deeply as I did, and Eatonville was just as much a part of her as it was a part of me, but even then I knew that it was in her to go. One day her mother's arms and a best friend would not be enough to contain her. Soon enough we'd be women, and I'd have to love my friend from afar while I stayed nestled in the bosom of my town.

I can't help but wonder how many other hearts — even those of folks who have never set foot in Florida — have bits and pieces of Eatonville in them now because of Zora's travels. It warms me from the top of my head to the tip of my toes to think that folks all across the world have the Loving Pine in their soul. It warms me even more to know that Zora, with all of her knowing might and her need to talk to the world, planted it there.

ZORA NEALE HURSTON

A Biography

To hear Zora Neale Hurston tell it, she was born in Eatonville, Florida, the daughter of a mayor, in 1901, or 1903, or 1910. Even from a young age, Hurston was an inventor of stories, a creator of masks and disguises. In reality, she was born in 1891 in Notasulga, Alabama, the fifth of eight children raised by John and Lucy Hurston. Her mother was a schoolteacher and her father a preacher and former slave (who did eventually become the mayor of Eatonville).

Although Alabama was her place of birth, Eatonville, Florida, was the place that truly felt like home to Zora. It was the first incorporated all-black township in the United States, established by twenty-seven African-American men soon after the Emancipation Proclamation. Hurston and her family moved to Eatonville when she was just a toddler, and the thriving community infected her with energy, confidence, and ambition. Hurston's childhood was idyllic.

But then in 1904, when Hurston was just thirteen, her mother passed away. Thus began what Zora would later call the "haunted years." Lucy Hurston had been the one to encourage her daughter to have courageous dreams. John Hurston encouraged his daughter, but just as often tried to tame her rambunctious spirit, sometimes harshly. After his wife died, John had little energy or money to devote to his children and grew detached from them emotionally. When he remarried, Zora and his new wife were like oil and water.

Zora left home after a vicious fight with the new Mrs. Hurston and struggled to finish high school while working a variety of different jobs. One of those jobs was working as a maid to a singer in a traveling theater troupe, an experience that sparked Hurston's love of performance, a passion that would last the rest of her life. In 1917, she found herself in Baltimore. She was twenty-six and still without her high-school diploma. So Hurston lied about her age, convincing the school that she was sixteen so that she could re-enroll and complete her education. From that point on, Hurston would always present herself as younger than she actually was.

In 1919, Hurston entered college, first at Howard University and then at Barnard College, where she was the only black student and studied under the famous anthropologist Franz Boas. During these years, her writing began to get recognized. Her first short story, "John Redding Goes to Sea," was published in Howard University's literary magazine in 1921.

In the 1920s, Hurston moved to New York City and became an integral part of the Harlem Renaissance, befriending poet Langston Hughes and singer-actress Ethel Waters, among many other cultural luminaries. Zora was the life of the party, frequently hosting artists at her home (though she retreated into her room when she needed to get any writing done).

In 1933, publisher Bertram Lippincott read Hurston's short story "The Gilded Six-Bits" and inquired as to whether Hurston might be working on a novel. Hurston answered yes—and then set to work writing one, which became *Jonah's Gourd Vine.* By 1935, Hurston had her first novel and a collection of southern folktales under her publishing belt.

In 1937, Hurston's most renowned novel, *Their Eyes Were Watching God,* was published. In that novel, Hurston's heroine, Janie Crawford, lives a conventionally circumscribed life until she chooses to break out of the mold and live only for herself. Much like Hurston, Janie has her eyes on the horizon and believes in a better life beyond it. The novel has been praised as a classic of black literature and a tribute to the strength of black women.

Hurston went on to write several other works, including a study of Caribbean voodoo practices, two more novels, and her autobiography, *Dust Tracks on a Road*. All in all, she wrote four novels and more than fifty short stories, plays, and essays. Sadly, Hurston never enjoyed any monetary reward for her success during her lifetime. When she died in 1960 at the age of sixty-nine, her neighbors had to take up a collection for the funeral. Hurston was buried in an unmarked grave in Fort Pierce, Florida, because the neighbors hadn't been able to raise enough funds for a funeral *and* a gravestone.

In 1973, a young writer named Alice Walker traveled to Fort Pierce to visit the burial site of the woman who had inspired so many black female authors with her courage and strength: Hurston had insisted on living life on her own terms during a time when many black Americans had been pressured to assimilate. "A people do not forget their geniuses," Walker said, and arranged to have a monument placed, at last, to honor the life and achievements of Zora Neale Hurston.

A Time Line of Zora Neale Hurston's Life

1891
Born in Notasulga, Alabama, the fifth of eight children, to John Hurston, a carpenter and preacher, and Lucy Potts Hurston, a former schoolteacher.

1894
The Hurston family moves to Eatonville, Florida, a small all-black community.

1897
Hurston's father is elected mayor of Eatonville.

1904
Lucy Potts Hurston dies.

1917–1918
Attends Morgan Academy in Baltimore, Maryland, and completes high-school requirements.

1918
Works as a waitress at a nightclub and a manicurist at a barbershop that serves only whites.

1919–1924

Attends Howard University and receives an associate degree.

1921

Publishes her first story, "John Redding Goes to Sea," in Howard University's literary magazine.

1925–1927

Moves to New York City and attends Barnard College as its only black student. Receives a bachelor of arts degree.

1927

Goes to Florida to collect folktales.

1927

Marries Herbert Sheen.

1930–1932

Organizes the field notes that become *Mules and Men.*

1930

Works on the play *Mule Bone* with Langston Hughes.

1931
Breaks with Langston Hughes over the authorship of
Mule Bone.

1931
Divorces Sheen.

1934
Publishes *Jonah's Gourd Vine,* her first novel.

1935
Mules and Men, a collection of folklore, is published.

1936
Awarded a Guggenheim Fellowship to study West
Indian *obeah* practices.

1937
Visits Haiti. While there, writes *Their Eyes Were Watching God* in seven weeks.

1937
Their Eyes Were Watching God is published.

1938

Tell My Horse is published.

1939

Receives an honorary doctor of letters degree from Morgan State College.

1939

Marries Albert Price III. They are later divorced.

1939

Moses, Man of the Mountain is published.

1942

Hurston's autobiography, *Dust Tracks on a Road,* is published.

1947

Goes to British Honduras to research black communities and writes *Seraph on the Suwanee.*

1948

Seraph on the Suwanee is published.

1956
Works as a librarian at Patrick Air Force Base, Florida.

1958
Works as a substitute teacher at Lincoln Park Academy in Fort Pierce, Florida.

1959
Suffers a stroke and enters the St. Lucie County Welfare Home.

1960
Dies in the St. Lucie County Welfare Home. Buried in an unmarked grave in Fort Pierce.

ZORA NEALE HURSTON

An Annotated Bibliography

The Complete Stories (1995)
Published after her death, this collection features
Zora Neale Hurston's short fiction, which was originally published in literary magazines during her lifetime. Spanning Hurston's writing career from 1921
to 1955, the compilation showcases the writer's range,
rich language, and development as a storyteller.

Dust Tracks on a Road (1942)
Hurston's autobiography tells the story of her rise
from poverty to literary prominence. The writer's
story is told with imagination and exuberance and
offers a glimpse into the life of one of America's most
esteemed writers.

*Every Tongue Got to Confess: Negro Folk-Tales from the
Gulf States* (2001)
Originally collected by Hurston in 1927, this volume
of folklore passed down through generations offers

a glimpse of the African-American experience in the South at the turn of the century.

Jonah's Gourd Vine (1934)
Hurston's first published novel. Based loosely on her parents' lives, it features a preacher and his wife as the main characters.

Moses, Man of the Mountain (1939)
An allegory based on the story of the Exodus and blending the Moses of the Old Testament with the Moses of black folklore and song. Narrated in a mixture of biblical rhetoric, black dialect, and colloquial English.

Mule Bone: A Comedy of Negro Life (1930)
A collaboration between Hurston and Langston Hughes, this comedic play is set in Eatonville, Florida, and focuses on the lives of two men and the woman who comes between them. Due to a copyright disagreement between Hurston and Hughes, the play was not performed until 1991.

Mules and Men (1935)
Gathered by Hurston in the 1930s, the first great

collection of black America's folk world, including oral histories, sermons, and songs, some dating as far back as the Civil War.

Seraph on the Suwanee (1948)

A novel that explores the nature of love, faith, and marriage set at the turn of the century among white "Florida Crackers."

Tell My Horse: Voodoo and Life in Haiti and Jamaica (1938)

Hurston's travelogue of her time spent in Haiti and Jamaica in the 1930s practicing and learning about voodoo ceremonies, customs, and superstitions.

Their Eyes Were Watching God (1937)

The most widely read and highly acclaimed novel in African-American literature and the piece of writing for which Zora Neale Hurston is best known. Tells the story of Janie Crawford as she develops a sense of self through three marriages and grows into an independent woman.

Children's Books Adapted from Folktales Collected by Zora Neale Hurston

Lies and Other Tall Tales. Adapted and illustrated by Christopher Myers. New York: HarperCollins, 2005.

The Six Fools. Adapted by Joyce Carol Thomas. Illustrated by Ann Tanksley. New York: HarperCollins, 2005.

The Skull Talks Back and Other Haunting Tales. Adapted by Joyce Carol Thomas. Illustrated by Leonard Jenkins. New York: HarperCollins, 2004.

The Three Witches. Adapted by Joyce Carol Thomas. Illustrated by Faith Ringgold. New York: HarperCollins, 2006.

What's the Hurry, Fox? and Other Animal Stories. Adapted by Joyce Carol Thomas. Illustrated by Bryan Collier. New York: HarperCollins, 2004.

ACKNOWLEDGMENTS

This book owes its existence to the Zora Neale Hurston Estate for generously endorsing our work; Lois Hurston Gaston and Lucy Hurston for trusting us with one of the most precious of life's gifts: a truly beautiful family legacy; Victoria Sanders, our brilliant and wickedly funny Xena warrior of an agent; Mary Lee Donovan, our dream editor, who saw our potential and added so much grace to our story; Richard Simon, for reading every word, lending his brilliance at a moment's notice, and generally making every page sing louder; Drew Baughman, for giving this story—with his companionship and love of nature—its candlelit skies and its swollen heart; Hildegard McKinnon, for being our tireless reader and supporter; Abou Farmanfarmaian, for reading and editing and believing; Mark Siegel, for his loving encouragement; Melanie Gerald, for her encyclopedic empathy; Robert Burnett Jr., for owning fully how he sees the world; and Zora Neale Hurston herself, for giving to the world an inexhaustible store of story, language, and thought that has nurtured and sustained us for all these years.